LEAK
Passage of Evil

L Bailey Bastian

ISBN: 978-1-7363398-0-0

DEDICATION

This book is dedicated to my husband, Scott Bastian, who never imagined that his 'what if' scenario about a pen would lead to this three-part dark fantasy fiction.

CHAPTERS

CHAPTER ONE

"She's dead," said a stunned eighteen-year-old girl to paramedics as they approached her. "I think she killed herself."

She was standing in the driveway of a woman she barely knew with a look of shock, unable to believe what had happened. Her sixteen-year-old sister stood beside her, speechless. The paramedics continued past the girls and into the garage where a woman in her mid-forties laid lifeless on the ground. It did not matter how quickly help arrived, she had been dead for hours.

"We found her in her car. I pulled her out," she added, following the paramedics into the garage, and wiping tears from her puffed eyes.

Neighbors began to migrate onto the sidewalk at the sight of emergency units on their street. They tried to get a glimpse inside the garage but the glare from the rising sun blocked their view.

"The car was still running?" asked a policeman, walking to the girls. His name was Roland. "Other than her body, did either of you touch or move anything? What are your names?"

"Yes, it was still running. I'm Carla and this is my sister Olivia," she answered as chills from being so close to the dead woman filled her body. "We didn't move anything but her body from the car. She was in the passenger seat. I touched the door and I turned the car off."

Roland was an average looking thin man in his thirties who stood under six feet. He guided both girls out of the garage and onto the driveway.

"I'll need you two to hang out for a bit so that I can get a statement," he said. "I'll be back shortly."

Roland walked back into the garage where paramedics were covering the body with a blanket.

"You'll need to leave her body here. I've called for the coroner," he said to the men.

"It looks like she killed herself," said one of the paramedics. "The only odd thing is that she's got a good size cut on her cheek. You may want to check inside the house, maybe she fell. There's no blood out here."

"Thanks, I'll do that."

The paramedics walked away leaving Roland alone with the body. He knelt and pulled the cover from her. She was dressed in a sweatshirt, stretch pants, and white sneakers. He looked at her face and examined the cut that the paramedics mentioned. He sighed, placed the cover back over her, and stood.

He stepped into the house from the garage wearing gloves and immediately noticed a handbag draped across the handle on one of three luggage bags. He opened the handbag, pulled out a wallet, and removed a driver's license. He kept the wallet in his hand along with the license and walked back outside to the girls who discovered the body. They sat on the hood of their small car, still in dismay and anxious to leave.

"Ladies, thank you for waiting," he said, looking at the identification from the wallet. "How do you know Sara Malor?"

"She responded to our door hanger to clean her house. When she first moved in, she hired us to clean it before she unpacked," said Carla. "Then she asked us to come once a week to dust and vacuum."

"How long ago did she move in?"

"A couple months ago," Carla replied, looking at her watch.

"Tell me what happened."

"We got here at six this morning and... and," answered Olivia who was still visibly distraught.

"Soon as we walked in, we smelled the exhaust, but we didn't know it was exhaust until we got close to the door leading to the garage," said Carla. "And there she was. We opened the garage door and then I pulled her out of the car, but she was already dead."

"There was a hose in the window. She killed herself," Olivia added in a fog. "I can't believe this."

"Did she seem okay to you the last time you saw her?" Roland asked.

"For just meeting her, she seemed fine," Carla answered. "I wonder why she would want to do that. How did she get that cut on her face?"

"I don't know but investigators and the coroner will figure it out," said Roland. "Can you think of anything that can help us in terms of her state of mind?"

"Like Carla said, we didn't know her well enough."

"We have other homes to clean and we're way behind. Though I'm not even sure we'll get to the other homes today. This is really creeping us out. Can we go?" Carla asked.

Roland nodded. "I have your information and if we have any more questions, we'll contact you. Thank you for staying," he said, with a nod as he turned and walked back into the garage.

# # #

Another hour passed and the investigation was near complete. The woman was placed inside a body bag and laid on a gurney. An attendant slowly rolled her body from the garage, down the driveway, and to the awaiting coroner's van.

Sara lived alone in a small community of middle-class families where everyone kept mostly to themselves. No one knew the woman who had only lived there a short amount of time before her fate of death struck her.

Neighbors continued to stand in the middle of the street watching, most still in their pajamas shivering from the brisk air, refusing to look away. They stepped back to the curb once the van was ready to leave and when it passed, they walked back onto the road even though there wasn't much left to see other than a photographer who was packing his camera and a new white luxury car with all four doors open.

As the photographer swung his camera bag over his shoulder and walked out of the garage, a casually dressed confident-looking man strolled inside. His name was Detective Grant Stockton, a muscular black man in his mid-thirties who stood just over six feet. He was followed by Roland who walked quickly to catch up to him.

"Grant, hey," Roland called. "I was expecting to see you at least an hour ago."

"I got tied up on the other side of town. I heard this was suicide, then recognized the address. Is that what you think?" Grant asked in a confused state, looking around inside the garage.

"Evidence shows that it was suicide," said Roland, shaking Grant's hand.

Grant frowned. "Then why did I see a crime scene vehicle pass me just as I arrived?" he questioned, staring at Roland. "I heard the call for several responders. And I didn't ask what the evidence shows, I asked what you thought."

Roland walked towards the corner of the garage, gesturing for Grant to follow.

"We need to collect evidence and do a thorough investigation, you know it as well as I do," Roland explained.

"Roland, you and I are the only ones who know exactly who this victim is. We know the probability of this not being suicide, right? Just you and I, so let it be suicide for now. I need time to do my investigation. I want this."

"Right, Grant, look, it appears she killed herself, but I don't control this, we have to handle this like any other. We have to rule out everything else, including homicide. I know you want to single-handedly take down the man that probably did this or had this done."

"She came to me man, she came to me for help. Now she's dead."

"And if someone did this to her and you know for a fact who did it, then you need to report it. This could help the FBI nail this guy."

Grant sighed deeply before looking at the car. "My heart almost fell into my stomach when I heard the address. Damn it! Is this my fault?"

"No reason to blame yourself," insisted Roland.

"How long had she been dead before she was found?"

Grant asked, walking closer to the car with Roland following.

"She was dead long before we arrived. Six hours possibly. A couple of cleaning girls found her around six this morning. They saw her in the car with the hose attached to the exhaust and pulled her out."

"Did she leave a note?" he asked in a suspicious tone.

"We haven't found one, but it is almost consistent with suicide."

"Almost?" Grant questioned. "What makes you say that?"

"There was a cut, a gash on her cheek. It was pretty deep, but we didn't find anything that may have caused it out here or in her house," Roland claimed.

"Someone else was here, maybe they struck her across her face, knocked her out, and put her in the car," Grant suggested.

"The coroner will have to tell us what could have caused it. The pattern of the cut was an arc, maybe some sort of knife. There's nothing that indicates that she hit her face against anything," Roland added. "Can't find any blood anywhere."

"He got to her," said Grant with sorrow, walking around the garage. "Listen, thanks for offering to help me out. She was clear that she didn't want any protection."

"And like any other time, we should have ignored her wishes and kept her safe."

"I'm getting too close thanks to her and he knew it. I'm calling bullshit on suicide."

"What are you going to do? This guy is no joke and slippery as an eel. Maybe you should turn over what you've learned or at least loop everyone in. Now is not the time to be the hero."

"If I were the hero, she'd still be alive," Grant

commented.

"The FBI needs that information," Roland lectured.

"What she gave me is keeping me a step ahead, I'll turn it over, but not just yet," he said in a cocky tone.

Roland could only shake his head listening to the arrogance of his friend.

"Unless you give them that information, her death is going to be ruled a suicide," said Roland.

"I'm aware," he responded. "She had a plan, Roland. She should have been on her way out of the country, not in a body bag. She didn't kill herself."

Grant strolled towards the door leading inside the house. He slipped on gloves before entering the potential crime scene, then stepped through the kitchen and into the family room gazing in awe at the beautiful Spanish designs from artifacts to the lavish pictures that were sitting on the floor below where they were to be hung. There were several unpacked boxes throughout the house.

He looked at the fireplace and could still smell the ashes from the flame that had died out. A glass filled with wine sat on an end table beside an over-sized chair partially covered with a blanket. Grant looked closer to the glass. Roland joined him.

"What are you thinking?"

"This glass. Doesn't look like she took a sip of it."

"So?"

"She's got a cozy blanket on the chair, she starts a fire with a glass of wine, relaxing before heading to the airport, and then all of a sudden she decides to go into the garage, in the middle of the night, somehow get a cut on her face and kill herself? This isn't making sense," he said, walking past Roland and to the door. "We know what this is. She didn't think she was being watched and she didn't think he'd find out that she came to me. This is murder," Grant declared, walking out.

CHAPTER TWO

The grounds of the juvenile rehabilitation center were clean and welcoming even though it was a boot camp for bad kids. Unruly teens and preteens were sent to the center as a last chance to straighten out their lives, and if that didn't work, the next step would undoubtedly be jail or prison. The center sat in the middle of nowhere, one-hundred miles from the nearest city. The landscaping was impeccable, and each cabin was graciously spaced apart from the other, making it look more like a wilderness resort. The grounds were split into sections where in some areas, teens were led in vigorous exercise by fierce counselors screaming commands. No one smiled, how could they? At the end of each day, they were sore, hungry, and tired, and they deserved every bit of the one month stay in what they called hell.

Sydney Gaines and Aubrie Johnson were at the end of the thirty-day process. It was lunch time and the group was wrangled into the food quarters where they sat so crammed together that they could hardly lift their arms.

There wasn't much talking and most of what could be heard was the sound of plastic spoons clanking on food trays.

Sydney was the only one not eating. Instead, she looked around in boredom, frequently pushing her long thick black hair from her face.

"Syd," said Aubrie with her mouth full of spaghetti, looking down at Sydney's full plate. "It tastes awful but at least it's food. You should eat."

Sydney pushed her plate away from her, causing Aubrie to glance at her and frown.

"I haven't seen you eat at all since we have been here," Aubrie commented, "You're making this so much harder than it has to be. Why won't you eat? It's like you're on a food strike. We've had worse. Plus, you need your strength, I don't even know how you haven't passed out."

The girls were both small framed and stood under five foot four. Aubrie was Caucasian, but Sydney wasn't sure exactly what her ethnicity was since her father was never identified. At first look, she appeared to be partially Hispanic and African American.

"I'm good and nothing is worse than this," Sydney grunted.

"If you don't want it," said a soft female voice from the other side of the table. "Can I have it?"

Sydney slid her plate to the girl. "It's yours."

As the girl reached for the plate, a slightly overweight female counselor approached.

"One serving per person," she snapped as she pushed the plate back to Sydney.

Sydney sneered at the counselor. "I said she could have it."

"That's too bad, Sydney. You need to eat your own food. No sharing," she ordered with a raised voice.

Sydney slowly began to stand when Aubrie grabbed her arm.

"What are you doing?" she whispered as Sydney snatched her arm away.

"Sit down Sydney!" scolded the counselor as she stepped closer attempting to intimidate her. "Remember, you wouldn't even be here if you didn't make bad choices! Don't let this be another one of those choices you will regret."

She was not bothered by the woman's comment. She glared up and down at her with a disgusted look before lifting her plate.

"What if I offered this to you?"

"Put the plate back on the table, sit down, and eat. I'm not going to tell you again!"

"This looks like a bunch of straws," she laughed. "Probably tastes like it too. What do you think?"

Sydney slammed the plate on the top of the counselor's head, catching the attention of the girls from other tables. Some began to giggle while others watched in excitement.

"Not that you need anything to eat, you fat bitch!"

There was sudden silence as the counselor wiped the spaghetti from her head. She gestured for a couple of male counselors to join her.

"By the way, I don't regret any choices I've made," Sydney snarled.

"Take this one back to her cabin please," the counselor requested in a calm tone.

Sydney looked at Aubrie and grinned. Aubrie could only sit in confusion by Sydney's actions. From the moment they arrived at the camp, Sydney's attitude was bitter and worsened as the weeks passed. Nothing nor anyone could please her and Aubrie was finding it more difficult to keep her calm. What was going on with Sydney, Aubrie questioned as she watched the male counselors escort her out along with the female counselor who was still brushing spaghetti from her clothes.

# # #

Since young Riley Rucker's untimely and gruesome death, Park Saire was never at ease. Day after day he waited for the one odd suicide that would bring him closer to finding the doll that carried the curse, the evil that changed the course of his life. He remembered scrambling through the creek where Riley threw the doll, desperately trying to pull it from the current that swallowed and washed it away. The doll was gone, and he knew that one day soon it would wind up in the hands of another unsuspecting victim. He could only pray that the new host of the curse wasn't far.

Memories of Frank flooded his head every day and, in a way, he had become him, looking for something that seemed untouchable. He kept his police radio on and for weeks, he made sure to watch the morning, noon, and night news, hoping not to miss a single reported suicide case.

Every case that he heard of in the surrounding cities and counties, piqued his interest and he thoroughly investigated each one until he was confident that there was nothing suspicious about the deaths.

There wasn't a routine or particular moment that triggered Park to replay the moments that led to where he stood. It was all so clear, and he would never forget the phone call that directed him to the hospital on the night that he met Frank. His mind constantly flashed back to when he heard the anguish in Frank's voice as he told him about the curse.

Visions of the rage that he saw in Riley's eyes as he and Frank fought her played over and over in his head. At times he wished he had never learned about the curse. But, had he not, he would have never known the truth to his sister, Piper's death. He recalled the second that he became convinced that humanity was being plagued by a demon from another world. He remembered the promise he made to Riley's mother, Quinn, and the horror that broke her.

He knew that Quinn would never be the same. Convincing her to leave the life she once had was simple, she wasn't happy before the terror began but she never imagined she would lose part of her family the way that she did. Quinn and her son, Dylan would never forget what happened to Riley and Gavin, and they vowed to never speak of it. Who would believe them? Ashley, the babysitter, was the luckiest of all, Park said to himself. Quinn saved her with her blood and reversed the curse along with her memory of Riley's attack.

Park was determined to keep his promise and he would not rest until Ostar and the curse was stopped.

Since his sister's death, his compulsive need for tidiness diminished along with his personal grooming. His only focus was on the curse and he was paralyzed to everything else. Unopened mail buried the table at the entrance of his home, dirty dishes occupied every room and his laundry basket had become his new dresser that sat in the middle of the bathroom.

In a matter of weeks, Park's weight dropped and his once tan skin turned pale. He had not gotten his thick and shiny black hair cut in weeks and it grew long enough to wear in a small ponytail. His sleep was constantly interrupted by the horror that was whirling in his head causing deep dark circles around his eyes. He wanted everything that he saw and experienced to simply be a bad dream, but when he opened his eyes, he was brought back to reality.

That morning the regular news was interrupted by a special broadcast. Park bit into a donut as he anxiously watched the banner that appeared at the bottom of the screen that read 'Woman found in car from apparent suicide'. As the broadcaster was about to speak, Park heard a knock on his door. He shoved the remainder of his food in his mouth, wiped his hands on his jeans, and paused the broadcast. He walked to the door curious as to who it was and slowly opened it enough to see that it was his fellow detective and friend, Milo Savatt dressed in a casual shirt, a light jacket, and jeans which was the only attire he had in his closet. He stood with his arms crossed carrying a folder in his hand. Park opened the door wider.

Milo last saw Park when he helped wrap up the incident at the Rucker house which was when Park decided to take a leave of absence. Unlike Park who had let himself go, Milo maintained his lean five-foot-ten physique along with a new look of a shaved head.

"What are you doing here?" Park questioned as Milo stepped in.

Park turned and slowly walked towards the kitchen.

"You want some coffee?" Park asked.

"Nah, I'm good," he replied, following Park. "Man, you need to open up some windows in here."

"I almost didn't recognize you. Nice look," Park said, ignoring Milo's comment.

"Thanks, early hair loss runs in my family. May as well stay ahead of it," Milo replied, rubbing his hand over his head. "I see you have a new look too, what's up with the grunge look and the bun?"

Park chuckled. "Isn't a bun up higher?" he asked,

pulling his thick hair into a higher ponytail.

"Good thing you have the face for that," Milo joked before becoming serious. "I haven't heard from you in a while, you won't answer my calls and I need to talk to you. I have something that I want to share with you. But I'm not so sure how to say it without you thinking that I'm crazy."

As Milo passed the small dining room, he noticed that it was converted into workspace with papers and photos neatly stacked over the table. There was a large corkboard on the wall with victims of the suicide cases that Park told Milo about.

Park opened the nearly bare refrigerator.

"Want some water or juice? Bloody Mary?" he offered, quickly pulling up his jeans that were no longer a perfect fit.

"I'll take some water," he said with a grin that showed deep dimples on both sides of his face. "You look like death. You okay?"

Park grabbed two bottles of water from the refrigerator and slid one across the island to Milo.

"I'm fine," he responded, reaching for a small bottle of pills that sat on the island. "Nothing a bit of rest won't cure."

"You've dropped quite a few pounds too. What the hell kind of diet are you on? You seriously can't afford to lose any more weight."

Park chuckled, shaking three pills from the bottle into his hand. "Not on a diet, just overly focused you could say. Enough about me, what's up?"

"What do you have going on in your dining room? Looks to me like you're doing some investigating on your own of those people that you told me about. You said it was probably nothing. Yet here you are."

Park tossed the pills in his mouth and washed them down with water. Milo raised an eyebrow, causing a moment of awkward silence.

Milo was Park's closest friend and he desperately needed someone to trust him and to believe in the unthinkable. Park was exhausted and when he tried to sleep, his mind raced along with his heart and before he knew it, it was morning and time to continue his quest.

Milo placed the folder that he carried on the island, slid out photos, and laid them side by side. Park walked to the other side of the island and examined the photos, taking an extended look at a picture of Piper.

"Why are you bringing these to me?" Park asked.

"This is something beyond real and you're going to think I am crazy," he said, pointing to each of the photos. "You wouldn't be still looking into this if it were probably nothing, no one but you noticed the similarities, the cut on their faces. And then there's the young girl, Riley, and the college girl Lacey, oddly enough neither had cuts on their faces, but both had faint marks on their right hand. Identical."

"Yes, I know, and you've said it twice now that I'm going to think you're crazy," Park said, folding his arms. "What are you getting at?"

"We've known each other for what, eight years?"

Park nodded.

"There's something that you never knew about me. When I was growing up, my parents would always tell me that if I did something bad, the Boogeyman was going to get me."

"Yeah well, I think all of our parents have said that at some point growing up," Park replied.

"Most kids don't take it literally," Milo said with a pause. "I did. Just the fear of seeing this Boogeyman kept me from doing anything wrong. All my friends would do this stupid kid stuff, one in particular called ding dong ditch. When it was my turn, I ran away because I knew it was wrong and that the Boogeyman would be waiting for me if I did it."

"Wow, did your parents realize how it was affecting you?"

"Not really, they just thought I was this perfectly good kid. They weren't even concerned when I avoided Halloween like the plague. Ghosts and goblins in my mind are real, they are evil and it's what makes people evil," he said, staring into Park's sunken eyes before finally blurting, "All of this, these people that have committed suicide... Evil made them do it and I think that something was inside of Lacey and Riley that allowed them to take over the minds of people and forced them to end their lives. Whatever was in them, it was put there by the devil."

Park's eyes widened with curiosity. "Devil?" he questioned, rubbing his hand across his unshaven face.

Milo picked up his bottle of water and walked into the dining room, stopping in front of the table where Park's pictures were stacked. Park, still in disbelief of what Milo said, followed him.

"Something is happening and it's not good," said Milo. "I can't find anything... yet... to prove it, but those two, Riley and Lacey, they were carriers of something and those marks on their hands had something to do with it. I visited the families of those who had some sort of interaction with Lacey. Not one of them can fully accept that their loved ones committed suicide, you couldn't even accept that Piper killed herself. Like the guy who walked into oncoming traffic on the freeway seconds after getting into an argument with Lacey. What made him do it? Why would he kill himself over a small fender bender and a shouting match? He had no mental issues, he was perfectly healthy. Why would he do what he did?"

Park was surprised. "I can't believe you went as far as finding the families. Did any say why they didn't come forward and talk to the police about it?"

"They each said that they didn't have any proof that would explain otherwise."

"Did you tell anyone about this?" he asked.

"I took it to the Captain. Showed him the photos and told him I thought we needed to take a closer look," said Milo. "But I didn't tell him my theory. He would have put me on leave and made me see a counselor, and then get cleared before I could come back to work."

"Let me guess, the captain said there wasn't enough to prove anything but coincidental suicides," Park concluded. "What about the cut on their faces?"

"He said that the injuries they sustained made it unlikely to prove that the cuts were the same," he explained, speaking quickly. "Like the one who blew out his brains, the man who ran his car into a tree, and even your sister's injuries. He said there wasn't enough of anything to tell that the cuts were even similar. As for the marks on both Riley and Lacey's hands, he chalked it up to some sort of new trend of crazy tattoos that these young kids are getting. He dismissed everything."

"It's just as well, the police can't handle this," said Park. "No one can handle what has come, not in the traditional way."

Milo held up a photo of the dead man from the car crash. "This is the guy who ran his car into a tree, the case was assigned to you because there was a shit load of money in the trunk of his car and you were trying to find a connection between that money and the company that he worked for, Rucker International. Gavin Rucker was the CEO and his adopted daughter was Riley Rucker. You were not telling me the truth."

Milo placed the photos on the table and lifted a photo of Riley's body that was taken in her backyard after she took her life.

"So, am I right? Do you believe that it is some sort of evil too?" Milo nervously asked, hoping that Park wouldn't think he was out of his mind. "I've been looking for Riley's mother Quinn to shed some light on all of this. You gotta tell me the story. All of it. What's going on?"

"Quinn is gone," Park said. "She took her son and went off the grid. I have no idea where she went."

"Why? I want to hear it from you. Why did she leave? What did she see? Tell me what happened."

Park sighed. "She saw hell, and you're right, I didn't tell you the truth about any of this. The guy that ran his car into a tree and the other man who blew his brains out kidnapped Riley for ransom. I couldn't figure out why they would both kill themselves after getting away with that kind of money but slowly the pieces came together. The money that was in the trunk of the crashed car was half of the ransom money. His partner was found in a cabin. They both had the same cut on their faces. I didn't think much of it either until I met Frank."

"And the other half of the ransom and is this the same Frank that was found dead at the Rucker house?" Milo asked.

"The money mysteriously made it back to the Rucker house. Riley told her parents that she found it in their driveway when in fact, she was at the cabin and caused the guy to kill himself. Riley was the cause of both of the kidnapper's deaths," he answered. "As for Frank, yes, I met him when I was called to follow up on a suspected child abuse case. A doctor thought that Riley's brother was being abused by their stepfather. Frank was at the hospital and tried to warn me that Riley was cursed and he needed help to stop her. Of course I didn't believe a word he said until later when he told me that his daughter, Lacey, held this curse before Riley. Lacey is the reason Piper is dead. It definitely is evil and both girls carried a... a curse."

Milo was relieved that Park confirmed his beliefs. "What kind of curse?" he asked.

"There's this ink that is in a pen. It's the blood of a demon... His name is Ostar. He is what is causing all of this. He is why this is happening. He needs human souls. Somehow it's supposed to bring life back to his world."

"His world? Ostar?" Milo questioned, confused.

"He's the evil that you speak of. I have not seen him. I've only heard his name over and over. When the blood leaks from the pen and onto the skin, they change, it's as if they are possessed. They make people kill themselves by cutting them on their cheek, always the right cheek. When they die, by suicide, their souls go to Ostar," Park explained. "The purpose of these carriers is to collect three souls for him. Once that third person's soul has gone to Ostar, the carrier will pass the curse to someone else and they will then take their own life. That is what happened to Lacey and Riley."

Park walked back into the kitchen and grabbed the photos that Milo had brought. He took them back to Milo.

Milo took a deep breath and exhaled. "What do we do?"

Park took the band from his ponytail and ran his fingers through his oily hair. "I'm not sure," he said, remembering that he had the news on pause. He walked back into the living room. Milo followed.

Park grabbed the remote. "This could be something," he said, pressing play.

"A 40-year-old Cliff County woman was found dead inside her car from an apparent suicide," announced the broadcaster. "According to police, the woman's house cleaners found her inside her running car with a hose attached to the exhaust pipe. The woman, identified as Sara Malor, was pronounced dead at the scene."

Park and Milo stood in front of the television speechless for a moment. Park paused the news station and looked at Milo.

"It's been almost a month since Riley died, I wasn't sure how far the doll could have made it, and now..."

"Doll?" questioned Milo.

"The pen, it's carried in this strange and odd-looking doll. We find the doll, we find the pen, and we find the carrier," Park revealed, putting his hair back into a ponytail.

"Guess we better get to work," said Milo, eagerly.

Park looked cautiously at his friend. "Are you sure? You came in asking me if I am okay but what about you? You talked about this stuff in passing and I know you are basically addicted to watching reruns of alien shows, but I am serious, this is serious and if you're here to humor me then..."

"How can I be humoring you, man? I brought this to you. I didn't even know how receptive you would be when I told you. I thought you were gonna kick me out of the house. When in fact, it's exactly what you're thinking," Milo lectured. "I really wish you would have been able to trust me and tell me what was going on."

"It's not every day that you hear your friend tell you about his belief in ghouls, goblins, and the Boogeyman.

Had I known, I certainly would have told you everything. That's a lot Milo. I'm thinking that doesn't go over well with the ladies."

"What ladies? I mean, what woman wants a man who believes in this stuff? That is what keeps me from even trying. I don't want to be labeled crazy so I don't dare tell anyone what I really believe. I'll wait for someone to come along that understands that this kind of thing is really happening," said Milo. "In my head, I knew there was truth to this and finally, there's proof to all of it. I'm right."

"I can't confirm that there's really a Boogeyman, but this is pretty darn close. I just can't believe what I'm hearing from you. Don't get me wrong, I'm glad, it's just hard to believe."

"The night Riley died, you wrote in your report that Frank was part of some botched robbery and was killed by one of his own men. Obviously, a lie. And you stated that these supposed robbers killed Gavin Rucker. Gavin had the same gash on his face. Riley did it didn't she?"

"Yes," he said as he recollected the events of that awful night. "I saw it with my eyes. Frank and I wrestled with her. Her strength was far beyond both of ours together. She had already sent Gavin's soul to Ostar and all that was left was for her to pass the curse and take her life. When we tried to stop her, she killed Frank," Park said, becoming agitated.

"I don't understand. Why our souls and why this way?" Milo questioned.

Park grabbed his car keys, wallet, and phone from the kitchen island.

"All I know is, according to Frank, that there is this realm... his kingdom, and every hundred years it needs twenty human souls by suicide and only through his carriers, five hosts to bring the dead from his world back to life," he said.

"Wow," Milo replied in deep interest.

"We can't risk ignoring what we just heard on the news. This could be it. The carrier may be closer than we think," Park said in haste, quickly walking to the front door and opening it. "Are you coming or not?"

Milo stood perplexed at what he heard from Park. Park closed the door and approached him.

"This is going to continue until he gets those twenty souls. I don't know the reasoning as to why only twenty but that is what Frank said. Honestly, I don't even know how many more souls have already been sent. This next carrier may be all that is needed, and we can't trust that if he gets that magic number, this will be over."

Milo heard the fear and pain in Park's voice and saw desperation in his face.

"Then we have to stop it," Milo said softly.

"If we can find out if Sara Malor has a cut on her face, then we would know for sure that the carrier is close, the next county over."

Milo sighed and walked out of the door ahead of Park.

"Let's go," he called back to Park.

CHAPTER THREE

Sydney sat on her lower bunk bed and leaned against the wall listening to the sounds of nature from the open window that was somewhat masked by the noise of outside activities. Apart from mealtimes, everyone spent most of the day in some sort of physical activity with counselors yelling commands. They were treated like the felons they were expected to become.

Each of the small cabins on the campground housed ten girls, all in bunk beds. The small space was by design because they were not expected to be in their rooms other than to sleep or in Sydney's case, to be used as a teen-aged version of time-out.

They were not allowed to bring any type of electronic device and were patted down before stepping into the van for the ride to the center and any devices found were immediately confiscated. Not being able to hear music made Sydney more anxious. She enjoyed listening to cafe music where most of the sounds were smooth and acoustic. It was calming and helped overcome the moments of her innate violence and lashing out. Since music was not an option, she found it more difficult to control her temper against the staff and other campers, not fully realizing that her new attitude was partially being driven by what was now inside her.

Sydney stood from her bed and walked into the bathroom. She shut the door and stared at herself in the mirror that spanned across the wall. She knew something was happening to her and she could feel the jolts of energy run through her veins, and each time it happened, her mind became more and more occupied by the vision of what she had to do for Ostar. The one thing Ostar didn't anticipate was Sydney's reluctance in using her power quickly to send him three souls and ultimately, her own.

She held her right hand to her face, examining the bars with a smile suddenly appearing on her face. She began to hum as she exited the bathroom and strolled back to her bed. She bobbed her head to the beat of her own music that became louder so that she could not hear the outdoor noise until she was interrupted by Aubrie. Sydney smiled at her and watched as she sat at the side of the bed close to her.

"Why did you do that to the counselor?" Aubrie asked, combing her fingers through her thick dark hair. She licked her full lips. "That's extreme even for you."

"Is the beast still mad at me?" Sydney grumbled.

Aubrie chuckled.

"Wouldn't you be mad if someone dumped a plate of spaghetti all over your head and you were wearing white? Doubt the sauce stains are coming out of that. And stop calling her the beast. She's just doing her sad ass job."

Sydney laughed with Aubrie.

"Wouldn't you dump a plate of spaghetti over an old

hag that called you a loser?"

"She didn't say you were a loser, but close. Trust me, I am not defending her. I'll always have your back, but really Syd? Why can't you just go with it so that we can get through this? When we stopped to get snacks on the way here, we agreed we were going to be good, even if we had to fake it. What happened to our deal? It literally went out the window the second we got here," Aubrie said, getting comfortable on Sydney's bed. "And where did you run off to last night?"

Sydney looked at her as if she didn't know what she was talking about and did not respond.

"Come on Syd, we're practically sisters and this sister knows you probably better than yourself. You took off and I saw you creeping back in around 2 am. You have a boy on the side that you're not telling me about?" she joked.

"Okay Aubrie, that's more your speed," she laughed with a pause. "I just needed to get out of this hell hole. I can't believe we are stuck here."

"We're almost done. We survived hell. Plus, it's better than jail."

"Feels like jail," responded Sydney as she laid beside Aubrie, looking to the wood ceiling and the fan that moved slowly. "I didn't think faking all this was going to be this hard. I cannot tell them what they want to hear. It's not me."

"Do it for me then," Aubrie demanded in a stern tone. "I, for one, am not coming back here and I'm certainly not going to jail."

"If they gave out awards, you'd probably get 'best ass kisser' trophy," said Sydney with a chuckle.

"Whatever it takes," Aubrie replied, returning a smile. "We have to think more before we do things, Sydney. We tried to rob a store. On a dare! For me, this opened my eyes. What we did was far worse than all the other little shit we did. We should have stopped at tagging the corner market."

"Now we know what we can get away with," said Sydney with sarcasm.

"It's more like, we know how lucky we've been," said Aubrie.

"But we're so cute."

Both girls giggled before Aubrie's smile faded.

"We keep our heads down and do what we're told until we turn eighteen. The stuff we did is done and over, we can't keep getting into trouble. I just feel that our luck has run out."

"Not me. I feel a lot of luck coming to my future," Sydney joyfully said.

"What does that mean?" Aubrie asked with a frown.

Sydney sighed. "Nothing, never mind. Honestly, being here is better than being home with, Miss Kankles," Sydney said in a bitter tone.

Aubrie laughed. "Can you imagine if we ever said that to her by accident! We'd get thrown out of the last foster home there is. We've worn out all the others."

"Even if we said it on purpose, I doubt she'd even know what it meant. I really can't stand her."

"Two more years. It'll go fast and we will be on our own. We can write our own ticket... finally," Aubrie said with enthusiasm.

"I have my ticket now," Sydney replied, rubbing the marks on her hand.

"Where did you even find a permanent marker to put that on your hand anyway?"

"What are you talking about?" Sydney asked.

"Your hand, when we first got here you said that you

were just doodling with a marker. Did you get another marker? Whatever you drew on your hand is a lot darker," Aubrie pointed out, still looking at the marks.

"Oh yea," she replied. "I found one on the ground."

"Why do you keep coloring it?"

Sydney became annoyed. "What does it matter?"

"Okay, okay," Aubrie said, pausing before continuing. "When are you going to tell me where you took off to?"

Sydney rolled her eyes. "Really? Enough with the questions. I didn't go anywhere, it's like that old prison on an island in San Francisco. We're in the middle of nowhere. But if you must know, I went outside and sat on the grass, counted as many stars as I could, and fell asleep. That is it, boring. I woke up and came back in."

Aubrie humorously but suspiciously glared at her.

"And no one saw you, they roam this place like we're hardened criminals. I don't know if I'm buying that Syd. But okay," she said, rubbing her aching shoulders. "I hurt so bad. Why aren't you sore? When we have to do sit-ups in PE at school, you complain that your stomach hurts, now all of a sudden, you're this badass ninja. What gives? The workouts they make us do here are complete torture and you're getting through them with literally no problem."

"I honestly don't know, I guess I just want to get it over with. Mind over matter is what I've always heard."

"I'd love whatever you're taking," Aubrie said, sitting up, pulling her hair in a ponytail and giving a grin. "Time for our confessional meeting. This is such a joke, but like I said, I'll play their games. Anything to make this as painless as possible, if there is such a thing."

"Confessional meeting?" Sydney laughed, dragging herself from the bed. "Try an AA meeting. You go ahead. I'll be right there."

"Sure, I'll save you a seat," Aubrie said as she stood and strolled out of the cabin.

Sydney looked around the cabin and up to the ceiling remembering when she first met Aubrie. They were six years old when they were placed in the same foster home. When they were ten, they were sent together to another foster family, a family that had better success with raising problem children. The bond between the two was immediate. They were instantly drawn to one another along with the resentment and anger they had bottled up.

They were both born to drug-addicted mothers and at night while they were supposed to be sleeping, they would stay up and trade stories of what they could remember from their horrible lives before they met.

After several unsuccessful attempts to permanently place the girls, they were finally taken in by a widowed woman named Joan who had vowed to never give up on any child that was placed in her home. Joan was far more harsh than any of their previous foster parents. They lived there for only six months before they got into trouble and were sent to the rehabilitation camp.

Neither Sydney nor Aubrie believed that Joan was taking in troubled teens to truly help them find a better path. They figured that she was only doing it for the extra income. She was mean and managed to constantly find everything wrong with what they did. No matter how clean the dishes were or how good the floor was mopped, it never was to her satisfaction. She seemed to enjoy barking out orders. But, with a total of four foster kids with troubled pasts, no one thought twice about the foster mother's strict rules.

Sydney pushed her thick frizzy hair behind her ears, stood, and grabbed her duffel bag. She tossed it on the bed and unzipped it. Inside a pocket, she pulled out the doll that was given to her by the homeless woman and opened the back. She took the pen from the doll and held it up to study it. The ink immediately ran down to her hand making the marks already there, more defined. She closed her eyes and when she opened them, her pupils flashed for a moment along with the blood that covered the whites of her eyes.

She calmly put the pen in the back of the doll and gently slid it back into the pocket of her bag. Moments later, her eyes turned back to their normal hazel color. She stepped quickly out of her cabin and to the recreation room where a group of fifteen young ladies along with a female counselor sat waiting for her.

"Thanks for joining us Sydney, we didn't want to start without you," greeted the counselor enthusiastically, only for her smile to fade when she saw the look of displeasure on Sydney's face.

Sydney walked to Aubrie and plopped beside her in the open seat. Her uncaring demeanor was noticed by everyone.

"Took you long enough," Aubrie whispered.

Sydney ignored her.

"Sydney, why don't you tell us what is bothering you," coached the counselor.

"Not a thing," Sydney quickly declared, guardedly folding her arms.

"It doesn't appear that way. We have all shared a lot in this group, except you. Can you tell us what is wrong? I am hearing from several that you spend all your allowed free time sitting on the floor staring at the wall."

"What's wrong with that?" Sydney defensively asked.

"Is there something bothering you that you can share?"

Sydney glared at the counselor.

"Nothing is bothering me! How many times do I need to say that nothing is wrong? Can't you get that through your stupid head!" she shouted.

The counselor took a deep calming breath. "I know you don't think that this process is of any benefit to you but trust me, it works. And this is part of it. You need to be able to talk about your problems, what makes you angry, sad, happy, and how we as a group can help each other get rid of the bottled-up frustrations. The only way this process doesn't work is if you're not willing to open up, be transparent, and allow yourself to be part of it."

"Then I guess the 'process' won't work," Sydney grumbled.

Aubrie was shocked. She put her hand on Sydney's knee. "Syd, stop."

Sydney sprang from her seat and looked at everyone.

"Stop looking at me! None of you are any better than I am and you know it! Stop looking at me or you'll be sorry!"

Aubrie grabbed Sydney's arm hoping to calm her and sit her back down, but she snatched away and stormed out.

"Sydney!" yelled the counselor. "If you're not back here in three minutes you will be marked as uncooperative and you know what that means! This is your final warning and your last chance!"

"I'll get her, please just wait," Aubrie begged as she ran out after her.

"Sydney!" called Aubrie, running to catch up to her. "Sydney stop!"

Sydney stopped walking and abruptly turned to her. "What!"

"What's wrong with you? What happened? You were fine 10 minutes ago. I'm used to your flipping out over stuff, but you've taken it way too far. Would you just stop? We have to do this session or we'll be stuck having to come back to do it all over again. Now come on. You're going to screw this up for all of us!"

Sydney's face turned to anger. "Leave me alone!" she screamed, storming away, only for Aubrie to catch up to her and stop her again.

"You will thank me later Syd. Do you really want to come back here for a do-over just because you're having a tantrum?"

Aubrie gave a smile and a wink to Sydney who immediately calmed down and smiled.

"I hate you, you know," teased Sydney with a grin. "I don't have tantrums."

"I hate you more," Aubrie responded, wrapping her arm around Sydney's arm, and leading her back into the room. "And yes, you do have tantrums."

# # #

Later that day while the girls were in their cabins on a break, the alarm from the speakers outside the camp rang. It was time for another breakout of several groups to participate in their last workout. The calisthenic exercises were excruciating and many vomited before they were halfway into the routine. They were forced to do a grueling number of push-ups, sit-ups, rope climbs, and miles of running. If anyone stopped, the entire group would have to start the whole set over. No one wanted to be the cause of having to do more, so no matter how hard and painful, no one gave up, except for Sydney. For her, there was no pain, in fact, she felt nothing, and every day she finished first. She didn't sweat nor did any of the exercises exhaust her. Sydney could do everything quicker and easier than anyone, and during that last session, she decided that she had enough and did nothing.

"Sydney," yelled a female counselor. "Push-ups, Now!"

Sydney ignored the woman. She strolled to a nearby tree and leaned against it without a care.

"Everybody else, get started! Mr. Stanley is going to keep count," she said, gesturing for the young counselor to join.

The counselor cautiously approached Sydney who was biting her fingernails out of boredom.

"Sydney," said the counselor. "What's going on? You know that you have to do this, right? It's part of the process for everyone while you are here."

Sydney ignored her and continued biting at her nails and looking at her fingers.

The counselor became annoyed and sighed. "Look, Syd."

"It's Sydney," she snapped, interrupting her in an abrasive tone. "Only my friends call me Syd and I'm so sick of everyone saying that this is a process. Just call it what it is?"

"And what is that?" the counselor asked.

"Torture for the hopeless."

"It's only torture if you're not getting anything out of it and you're only hopeless if you feel that way," she said, before pausing to think of what to say next to the angry girl. "Okay, Sydney, I know you can do the exercises with extreme ease. It's quite amazing. You need to take this talent that you have and channel it into something positive, maybe a sport in school. You are very good and with that said, you still have to participate. If you don't, your peers will have to do even more. Is that fair?"

Sydney began pulling loose bark from the tree and tossing it on the ground. She refused to look at the woman.

"All I am asking is to just do the exercises. You don't even break a sweat, so please, help everyone else out. They are all trying extremely hard and I'd hate for them to be punished for your actions."

Sydney took a deep breath and exhaled. Without another word to the counselor, she brushed past her and back to her spot where the kids were still doing push-ups. She dropped to the ground and quickly did them, again finishing before everyone else. Sydney grinned at Aubrie who struggled to finish her push-ups. Once everyone was done, they laid on their backs on the ground trying to catch their breath before they would be ordered to do the next set of workouts.

"What the hell Sydney!" Aubrie exclaimed. "How are you able to do all of this so easily? When they made us run two miles, you were barely breathing! You are crazy good at this!"

Sydney and Aubrie laughed.

"You've been holding out on me. You should be on the cross-country track team," Aubrie suggested.

"No thanks," was all Sydney said as the counselors blew the whistle for everyone to begin again.

CHAPTER FOUR

Grant was at his desk in the detective unit of the police station studying notes he had taken on Sara Malor's death. All of his peers had partners and often sat in spaces beside or across from one another. It was not the case for Grant. He worked alone by choice and even moved his desk further away from everyone else. He was partnered with many throughout his six years as a detective, but his enormous ego and the need to control chased them away. Even the proud walk and cocky grin of the lone wolf alerted everyone that he was absorbed in only himself.

A woman in the department approached and stopped at his desk.

"Detective," she said.

He did not hear her. She tapped his shoulder. Grant nonchalantly turned to her and looked up.

"There are a couple of detectives from Frasier County looking to speak with someone about the Malor suicide."

Grant looked around the woman's waist to see Milo

and Park standing at the entrance. Park was holding the folder with the photos.

"Thanks, and it's the Malor investigation," he sternly said to the woman. "We haven't ruled it a suicide."

The woman rolled her eyes and walked away as Grant stood to meet the men.

"Well well, if it isn't Park Saire," said Grant with a smile, extending his hand to Park. "What brings you all the way out here? Last time I saw you was at the detective run up north."

"Yes, yes," Park said, recollecting the event. "I think I hurt for a week, maybe longer. Milo was there too."

Milo looked down and gave a shameful smile.

"That's right, hello Milo," said Grant with a chuckle. "That had to be the highlight of the run. Thirty minutes after the race was completely over, I saw you in tears being helped to the finish line by two women probably in their early seventies."

Park began to laugh. "They finished the race, then ran back to help you. I'm so sorry that I left you, man," Park said to Milo. "I wanted to at least finish the half marathon within the time allowed and try to beat this guy. I figured you would have just given up and taken a cab to the nearest pub."

"I saw a few along the way, but hey, I finished. That's all that counts," Milo said, shaking Grant's hand. "And it wasn't tears, it was sweat."

There was a moment of silence other than the clearing of throats.

"So, what can I do for you? How about a tour? We've got some pretty cool state of the art equipment that I know hasn't reached Fraiser County."

"Can we go somewhere and talk?" Park asked, becoming serious.

"Of course," answered Grant, curious to know what the men wanted from him. "Follow me."

The men walked down the corridor and to a small conference room. They sat at a rectangular table where Park slapped the folder on the table, immediately grabbing Grant's attention.

"We think the suicides in Frasier County are connected to your recent suicide. Or rather supposed suicide," said Park, opening the folder.

"Supposed?" Grant questioned, flipping through the pictures in the folder. "You think these random suicides in another county connect to the Malor death? How so?"

Grant closed the folder and handed it back to Park with no concern. Park opened the folder again, slowly flipping through the photos.

"These victims… look at their faces, I know some are hard to make out due to the circumstances of how they died, but you can certainly see the cut on their cheeks. They are all in the same arc pattern," he said. "Your victim, Sara Malor, if she has a similar cut on her face then they may somehow connect."

Grant raised an eyebrow and said, "I was told that she had a cut on her face, but her body was already removed by the time I arrived. I'll have to look at the postmortem photos to confirm, I should be getting them shortly. Cut or not, I know Sara did not commit suicide."

"Neither did these people," said Park.

Grant's eyes shifted from Park to Grant and then back to Park.

"I doubt that those people have any connection with Sara... unless there's an association between them and Holden Griggs."

"Griggs? You think he is behind your victim's death?"

"There could be a slight possibility that Holden Griggs

didn't have anything to do with Sara's death, but I doubt it, you do know who he is, right?" Grant asked.

"Who doesn't? We heard that the FBI and other agencies are working to get him and his operation off the streets. His drugs have made it into our county," Milo answered. "Are you working the Griggs case too?"

"Sort of," he quickly responded. "I'm going to tell you something and I trust you'll keep this to yourselves. Sara was in a relationship with this guy and I plan to be the one to put him away."

"And that's why you think Griggs had something to do with her death," Park concluded.

"I do. She's dead and he's the reason."

"That's quite the assumption," Park commented.

"You don't know the whole story," Grant replied in a defensive tone, standing. "The suicides in your county are probably just that. They aren't going to connect to Ms. Malor's death, I promise you that, and with that said, it's always good to see the competition."

Park sighed feeling defeated. He and Milo stood.

"Thank you for your time. Would you mind still letting us know if the cut on your victim's face is the same as our victims?" Park asked, pulling a card from his wallet, and placing it on the table.

"It won't prove anything, but sure," said Grant, picking up the card, then giving Park his card. "Park, on another note, you and I need to catch up, maybe over a few drinks the next time you're in the area. And Milo, I'll see you at the run next year, you may want to get started with building up your endurance."

The men chuckled. Grant walked the two men to the door and went back to his desk while Park and Milo slowly walked back to the car.

"He seems quite sure that Holden is behind Sara's

death," said Milo as they walked. "How do you know him, other than at the run? He throws off asshole vibes."

The two stopped on opposite sides of Park's car.

"We went to the same high school," Park replied with a chuckle. "He was three years ahead of me but I happened to be a whiz in math and I tutored him, of course it had to be hush hush. He didn't want it getting out that he needed help from a freshman. He paid me so I never said a word. He wasn't an ass, but his confidence was overbearing. I heard he was a detective out here but I never saw him again until we did the race. He hasn't changed and it doesn't shock me that he's after Holden Griggs on his own. Little does he know, we're about to go after him too… Holden Griggs is the carrier."

"What do you want to do?" Milo asked.

"We need to find him. Grant is hell-bent on being the hero and taking him down isn't going to be as easy as he thinks. Not even close," Park said, rubbing his temples as he closed his eyes.

"You okay?" Milo asked. "Headache?"

"Yea," replied Park. "I'm fine. It'll go away."

"You're going to follow Grant, aren't you?" Milo asked.

"I am," he said. "If anyone can find Griggs, it's going to be Grant. It's best I do this on my own, at least until I can confirm that he holds the curse. If anything goes south, I don't want the captain coming down on both of us."

"If he is the carrier, have you thought about how you're going to stop him?"

"I think about how to stop this whole thing since it began and I... I still don't know."

"What you should be thinking about is getting out of those clothes that you look like you've worn for days and getting yourself cleaned up."

Park rubbed his face and chuckled before getting into the car.

# # #

It was a quiet ride home from the rehabilitation center. The month was long and exhausting not only for the counselors who had to constantly reign in the teens but also for the kids who spent every moment of their time being counseled, forced into excruciating physical drills, and being told what to do.

Aubrie and Sydney were dropped off at their home just as it became dark. Aubrie walked ahead of Sydney and into the old two-story home, both dragging their bags behind them. Their foster mother, Joan, stood in the living room waiting for them to enter.

Joan was just a little over five feet tall and was slightly overweight. She had thick legs and calves which is why the girls secretly called her Miss Kankles.

"I hope you learned a few things at camp ladies. You two are incredibly lucky that you weren't put in jail for your latest stunt. When are you going to get your acts together?" she barked, pulling her bone straight short and thin hair behind her ears. "Go put your things away and get started on cleaning the kitchen."

Neither stopped to listen. They continued a slow walk up the stairs and to the bedroom that they shared. It was a small room with two twin beds on opposite sides of the room pushed against the dingy white walls. The carpet was worn from years of foster children residing there and the once white blinds were broken and stained.

"This sucks," Sydney grumbled as she tossed her bag on the floor and plopped on her bed. "I can't decide which is worse, the camp or this trash of a house. How can she let us live in this shit hole? She makes us mop and clean, and it does no good! With all the money she gets for us, she could use some of it to at least make it livable. Those social service people could care less about the filth that we are forced to clean up every day. We're not a thought in their minds or in Joan's. I can't stand her!"

"Who can? But this is it, Syd, no one else will take us after everything we have done. So just stop. We aren't going to find better," Aubrie argued, stepping close to Sydney and gazing into her eyes. "We just gotta keep telling ourselves, two more years."

"I had a plan, Aubs. It was a good plan."

"What are you talking about?"

Sydney walked away from Aubrie and faced the window, staring at her reflection.

"Nothing," she said, discouraged.

"We need to get down there and start our chores," Aubrie urged.

"We didn't even mess it up. We weren't even here," Sydney complained, covering her eyes with her hands. "I just wanna go to bed."

"It's barely past five o'clock Syd. I hate it when the time changes, it's too dark," Aubrie joked. "Come on, let's just get it done, then we can pass out."

"Or sneak out," Sydney hinted.

Aubrie held her hand out to Sydney and when she reached, Aubrie began to stare at the marks on her hand.

"Okay, so this just keeps getting darker," Aubrie commented in concern. "Why do you keep drawing on your hand? That can't be good for your skin."

Aubrie began to rub her fingers across the marks before Sydney pulled her hand away.

"Self-expression," Sydney replied with a grin. "Can't afford to get a real tat."

Aubrie frowned.

"You have been acting so strange. What's wrong?"

"Can we drop it Aubs? Let's go get this over with."

"At least tell me what it means? Four bars, one longer than the rest. What the hell? It looks like some weird giant bar code."

Sydney put her arms around Aubrie's neck and hugged her.

"If I stop doodling on my hand, will you stop with the interrogation?"

"Maybe if you wash it off, and please don't tell me that it means bars as in behind bars."

Both girls strolled out of their bedroom and into the kitchen giggling until they noticed Joan standing with her hands on her thick hips. She was in her late forties and never wore makeup on her cold hard face. She sized them up as they walked past and stopped at the sink.

"You rinse and I'll load," said Aubrie with a sigh.

"This is such bull," Sydney complained softly under her breath.

Sydney was so unhappy with dish duty that she began quickly rinsing and cracked a dish. Joan immediately noticed.

"Sydney, breaking things isn't going to make all of this go away. Next one you break you'll find yourself scrubbing more than just dishes," Joan bellowed. "And you better not miss those pots and pans on the stove!"

"I didn't do it on purpose Joan!" Sydney yelled back.

Joan rushed to Sydney, slapped her hand on her shoulder, and swung her around. "Don't you ever raise your voice to me!"

"Then don't give me cause... Joan," Sydney snapped in an evil tone.

Sydney glared at Joan, refusing to look away. Joan was

stunned. She never had anyone, no matter how undisciplined, speak to her in that manner. The look on Sydney's face was eerie and concerning. Joan's breathing became heavier while Sydney remained calm. Joan crimped her lips then turned and quickly stormed out of the kitchen. Sydney began rinsing the dishes again as if nothing happened.

"What was that?" Aubrie blurted. "I have never seen you talk to her like that. Ever. Fighting with Joan is going to backfire. We have to keep our heads down."

"She doesn't scare me. She needs to be very careful."

"I'm going to keep saying this until you start doing it. The deal. We made a deal to just go with all of this, no matter how much we hate it," Aubrie replied. "You can't threaten her."

"You have no idea what I can do," Sydney said with a smirk. "The deal is off."

"You're getting weird," Aubrie stated in disgust, tossing the dish towel that she held onto the counter. "Finish this on your own."

Aubrie walked away and up the stairs to their room.

Sydney chuckled with no concern before continuing with the dishes. She looked through the window above the sink, seeing her reflection again. Her smile disappeared as she studied the face that stared back at her. She knew she wasn't the same person that she was before the ink from the pen absorbed into her skin. Her mind was no longer hers, it belonged to something else that was urging her to complete her new journey. She watched herself, turning her head from side to side before giving a proud grin.

# # #

"Why are we walking so fast?" Aubrie whined out of

breath and practically running to keep up with Sydney.

"A whole month Aubs," Sydney grunted, marching down the partially lit street with her fists balled. "We're not wasting our first night back sitting in our room waiting for more orders."

"I know it's cold, but do you have to walk so fast? Slow down or I'm going back home," Aubrie complained, trying to keep pace. "We got out of the house, the warden didn't see us, so all we gotta do is get back before the sun comes up. Can we please slow down? What's the rush? Everyone will be there for hours!"

Sydney didn't respond to Aubrie, she kept walking quickly down the street. Aubrie abruptly stopped.

"Sydney. Stop!" Aubrie yelled to her as the distance between them became greater.

Sydney was annoyed. She turned and stormed back to her. "What? Come on!" she scolded, grabbing Aubrie by her arm, and pulling her.

Aubrie snatched away.

"What is wrong with you? We both said we were sorry about the whole thing that happened when we were doing dishes. I said I would sneak out with you and you're acting like you're still mad!" Aubrie cried. "I changed my mind, we should have stayed home. What if we get caught? I can't go back to that camp."

"I doubt sneaking out of the house measures close to hot wiring a car and trying to rob a store. You didn't have to come with me you know. You're starting to sound like a joke. Now, are you coming or not?" Sydney asked with little concern.

Aubrie contemplated what to do when Sydney suddenly smiled and tilted her head.

"Okay, okay, I'm sorry," Sydney said. "How about we stay for an hour and then head back. The warden won't even know we left."

Aubrie was confused by Sydney's constant and abrupt change in her emotions and mood.

"Please? We deserve this for surviving hell," Sydney convincingly said. "We deserve a night out. I know you agree."

Aubrie sighed. "Okay, but in an hour we head home."

Sydney giggled and hugged Aubrie, then grabbed her hand and ran to a house that was a block further down the street. They entered a large two-story home without knocking. Kids roamed around while others sat, having random conversations, and laughing. Most of the teens held red plastic cups filled with beer or alcohol. A keg sat in the dining room, and liquor and soda bottles covered the dining table.

Sydney and Aubrie both grabbed empty cups and stood at the keg waiting for their turn.

"Hey you two," said a boy, holding the nozzle to the keg.

He poured beer into Sydney's cup and gazed at her.

"Where have you been? You missed a few weeks of group chats and some good parties," he added.

"Boot camp for bad girls is what I heard," replied a red-headed girl named Amy who stumbled to them, spilling beer from her cup. "I'm trying to picture you two obeying orders that are literally being barked at you. No thanks."

Sydney looked at the girl in disgust while Aubrie gave a weak laugh, not finding what she said funny.

"The month felt like a year," Aubrie added. "Did anything exciting happen or any fun gossip spread while we were gone?"

"Same fun as always," Amy slurred as she sipped from her cup. "Hey, Sydney, Josh over there beat your record."

"What record?" Sydney questioned with a frown.

Amy started to uncontrollably laugh, losing her balance, and falling into Aubrie. "How many people he could piss off in one night."

Sydney saw no humor and walked away. Aubrie accompanied her.

"Just ignore her, she's just being her usual drunk self," said Aubrie. "Let's go out back."

Sydney hunched her shoulders and led the way through the kitchen, out the patio door, and to the back yard where kids sat in chairs around a fire pit. Each had a drink and passed joints around to one another. Aubrie approached the group then looked back to Sydney who stood with a sour look on her face. Aubrie walked back to her.

"What's wrong?"

"I think we should branch out," Sydney said in a cocky tone, loud enough for everyone outside to hear her. "I am so sick of... boring."

"What the hell does that mean?" a teen girl questioned in a defensive tone. "We all take risks to have these parties when our parents leave, and you have the nerve to knock us? You're lucky that we invite you, seeing that you have no parents, therefore, can't host a party."

Sydney chuckled. "Good one."

"That's such an unfair jab," Aubrie argued.

"It's no big deal. I'm sick and tired of seeing the same sad group of people. I want to go to a real party. A party where we're not judged by all of you privileged assholes. All you say is how good you have it and you make sure that we're somewhere close to hear it. Well, we're not jealous!"

Aubrie stood next to Sydney. "Knock it off Syd. Stop acting like this."

"This is pathetic and I'm glad I finally spoke up! I'm out of here!"

Sydney walked back through the house and swung the front door open surprised to see Joan standing on the porch, furious.

"Get in the car Sydney!" she shouted before looking in the background to see Aubrie. "You too Aubrie! Now!"

Aubrie didn't hesitate to scurry out of the door past Sydney and Joan, and to the car. She hopped in the back seat and shut the door, looking out the window at Sydney and Joan who were in a staredown.

"Now Sydney! I am at my last rope with you! Both of you! Go! Now!"

Sydney turned her head away from Joan as her eyes flashed a shimmer of light. Once it disappeared, she faced her again.

"I see that you don't have anything better to do than follow us," Sydney said with a smirk. "You're tracking our phones. I knew there had to be another reason why you would give us phones. Certainly not out of the graciousness of your heart, seeing that you don't have one."

"I should have done it a long time before you two decided to go out on your crime spree," she said with a look of disgust. "Get in the car."

"Gladly Joan, for once, seeing your ugly face is a relief," she said, brushing against her shoulder as she casually walked to the car and got in the back seat beside Aubrie.

Not a word was spoken on the short drive back to the house. Once they were home, both quickly got out of the car and hurried to their room before Joan could get into the house.

"Sydney. Oh my gosh! You're really going after Joan.

You gotta stop before she kicks us out."

"She's lucky that she didn't make me mad, I am so over her," Sydney said as she plopped face down on her bed.

Aubrie sat at the foot of Sydney's bed with a serious look.

"I'm starting to worry about you."

Sydney didn't say a word as she buried her head in her pillow.

"You've been acting pretty hostile since camp. You took off in the middle of the night and you're telling me that you were outside looking at the stars, but I am not sure if I can believe you. You know, you're not the easiest person to get along with and now you're going out of your way to get a rise out of everyone, including me. Are we even still best friends?"

Sydney slowly turned on her back and looked at Aubrie.

"I wish we were blood sisters Aubs," was all Sydney said in a depressed tone before she closed her eyes.

Aubrie sighed, stood from Sydney's bed, and walked out of the bedroom.

CHAPTER FIVE

The next morning, Park made the drive back to Cliff County to visit Grant. He hoped that Grant would have called him to tell him that he saw the cut on Sara's face in the photos and that it was consistent with his victims, but he also knew that he was not on Grant's priority list. Park was filled with anxiety and couldn't think of anything else but confirming that Holden Griggs was the carrier. He did, however, find it odd that someone like Holden would find enough interest in a doll, find the pen, and become cursed.

He walked into the detective division adjusting the clean t-shirt and jeans he wore, wishing he had worn a belt. He immediately saw Grant at his desk and approached him as Grant stood.

"Hello Grant," Park greeted, trying not to sound annoyed that he never called him.

"Park," said Grant. "You're back. I wish you would have called first. I'm not sure that I have the time later for that drink."

Park slapped his hand on his forehead and said, "I'm sorry, I completely forgot about that. I'm actually here about the photos. The postmortem photos of Sara Malor."

"Yes, right," he said, sitting at his desk.

He began typing on his computer keyboard.

"You have quite the concern. I already told you whether she had a mark or not on her face that it won't convince me that her death connects to your suicide cases. I highly doubt that your supposed victims were mixed up with this guy."

"Just humor me. What about the photos, did she have a gash on her face similar to those in the pictures that we showed you?" Park inquired with a sense of urgency.

Grant sighed as the postmortem photos of Sara appeared on his computer. Park peeked at the screen and gave a look of relief when he saw the cut on her face.

"Let me help you catch him," Park blurted, still focused on her face.

Grant looked around the busy department. "Follow me," he said, walking into the same small conference room as before.

Park immediately sat in the first chair at the table. Grant sat across from him.

"I don't need your help or anyone else's. Maybe if I tell you the story, you'll back off with your theories," he said, hesitating before he continued. "She came to me the day before she died with some valuable information. Her death was because the information was about Holden Griggs."

# # #

Sara stood at the entrance of the detective's unit anxiously waiting for someone to come and speak with her. She had something that she needed to share and the longer she waited the more she thought about turning and walking out. Fear was evident on her face and she couldn't stop herself from frequently looking over her shoulder until finally, Grant approached.

"Ms. Malor," greeted Grant. "I'm told that you need to speak with someone about a crime. I'm Detective Grant Stockton."

He extended his hand, noticing that she was trembling.

"What's going on? Can I help you?"

"Yes," she softly responded, looking directly into his eyes. "I am in a... was in a relationship with Holden Griggs and I have information that I am hoping will lead to his arrest."

"Please," he said, gesturing for her to walk with him. "Let's talk somewhere more private."

Grant sat her at a table in a small interview room. He left for a moment and came back with a cup of coffee and placed it on the table in front of her. She nervously rubbed her hands and interlocked her thin fingers.

Sara had a trim tall frame, wore modest makeup, and styled a short brown sassy haircut with wispy bangs that she continuously pushed from her face.

Grant sat and said, "When you say a relationship with Holden, was it a romantic relationship?"

She lowered her head in shame.

"Yes," she admitted. "It was. Honestly, with the kind of money he was flashing around, I knew he was into something bad, but I just recently learned how bad."

Grant raised an eyebrow. "How long have you been with him?"

"A few months and now it's over. How could I have been so stupid? He's putting drugs and God knows what else on the streets and it's killing people... kids. I can't stand by and let this happen."

"What information do you have?" he anxiously asked. "Tell me what you know."

"Do you believe that things happen for a reason?" she asked Grant.

Grant hunched his shoulders. He didn't believe in luck, good or bad, and he never believed that things happened for a reason, but what harm would it be to tell her that he did.

"Yes, I do."

"That's good, so do I, and I think I was meant to be with him so that I could bring this information to you. To stop him."

"I'll certainly do whatever I can Ms. Malor, to do just that. He's a powerful man and whatever you can tell me will help."

"He's meeting someone the day after tomorrow," she said.

"What kind of meeting?" Grant asked, jotting in his notepad.

"I'm not sure but I overheard him talking to someone about where to meet and what time. He also said to make sure he wasn't followed and something about business being business and that they can't afford for their product to be mishandled."

Grant finished writing and looked at her.

"What you're doing is brave. But it's also dangerous. How did you get mixed up with him? I'm curious about how you did not know who he was?" he asked. "The FBI has been trying to build a strong enough case to put this guy away for life for quite some time."

"Love is indeed blind," she said in embarrassment. "I met Holden in Spain. I had been living there for three years. He was vacationing, so he told me. He said his name was Holden Graham. I rarely kept up with what was going on in the United States and I had no idea that he was this drug trafficker until I came back, with him. He said so many hypnotizing words to me that I... I... Honestly, he could have given me his real last name, I wouldn't have known any difference."

She pulled a tissue from her purse and wiped her eyes that were filled with tears.

"He said I took his breath away and I fell in love with him at first sight. He rented a house for me here to be close to him," she said. "He wanted me to move in with him, but it was just too soon for me. He got more points just for understanding."

"And then you realized that he was mixed up with more than

you ever imagined," Grant confirmed.

"I spent a lot of time at his house. There was a folder sitting on the counter in his kitchen and when he went out, he left it there and I didn't think twice about reading what was inside. He wasn't offering any information about himself to me and I knew in my gut that he was into something illegal, even before I left Spain. But I didn't care. No one had ever swept me off my feet the way he did and I didn't care," she said with a sigh before continuing. "Anyway, I was still curious as to what he was up to and how he was making so much money. Those papers led to my breaking into his office. I found ledgers, accounts, payments to men for thousands of dollars. Men who are now mysteriously dead."

Grant could only listen and observe the fear on her face as she explained.

"I've got to be the biggest fool out there, but I swear, I did not know how bad it was until I found those papers and started to do research."

"Why didn't you come forward immediately?" Grant asked.

"He caught me going through his office and I confronted him about his true last name and who he really was. I confessed to him what I found and told him I would say nothing if he didn't stop me from going back to Spain. He laughed at me. He seriously thought that his showering me with money, paying for my rent, giving me a nice car and everything I could ever want would make me look the other way and stay with him," she cried, wiping the tears from her face. "He wasn't going to let me leave and I was afraid. If I told him no to anything he was offering, I knew it would be the end of my life, so I told him I would stay and say nothing."

"You've taken quite the risk by coming here," Grant stated. "Don't you think that he's watching you now?"

"I knew I was being watched but I also knew that I would have a chance if I just went along with him and convinced him that I wanted to stay. I even told him I wanted to someday marry him. A few days ago, that gut feeling that I had of being watched was gone

and I had to take the chance," she said, pulling out several documents from her over-sized bag. "Here, I took pictures of everything I could and got them printed. Is it enough to put him away? If the FBI is investigating him as you say, can you pass this information to them?"

Grant took the documents and quickly sifted through them.

"I will. You said that he's meeting someone in two days?" Grant asked.

She nodded.

"Yes, at eight. His schedule is in the folder."

"Is there someplace you can go? Somewhere Holden cannot find you? I know you think that he's not watching you, but it is possible that he still is. Your life can change the second you walk out of this station. Do not trust your feelings. Holden is more clever than that."

Sara gave a grim smile. "I have to trust my gut. I'm already packed and heading to the airport late tonight. He won't find me."

"I can't guarantee you that we will have him in custody right away, Sara. Everything you have given me is good evidence, but we need to go through this and make sure that we have enough to arrest him and get his operation off the streets for good," Grant said. "Holden is more dangerous than you know. Let me put a car outside your home just in case. I'd feel better if I knew you were safe."

"If Holden were to see or find out that a police car or any suspicious car was sitting outside my house, he'd know for sure what I have done," she said. "My flight leaves for Spain at five in the morning. I'll be in the air and on my way soon enough."

Grant sighed. "Okay, write down your number and address," he insisted, giving his note pad to her. "And your flight information."

Sara jotted her information on the paper, slid it across the table to him, and stood.

"I wish I could go back in time and just walk the other way."

Grant stood and escorted her out of the room. He placed a hand on her shoulder.

"Thank you for this. I'll be in touch."

As she walked away, Roland approached taking notice of the woman leaving.

"Hey Grant," Roland cheerfully greeted.

"You're awful bubbly, you already meet your ticket quota or something?" Grant joked.

"This is me, Grant! Mr. Bubbly! You should try it sometime. I wanted to see if you want to go with me to a poker thing."

"Sure, when?" Grant asked, paying more attention to the papers from Sara than Roland.

"Tonight," Roland quickly answered.

"Nah, I can't, it's a school night for me anyway," Grant responded. "I've got something big I am working on."

"Holden Griggs, I assume."

Grant nodded. "Remember, not a word. Something just fell in my lap and I plan to get this guy on my own."

Roland chuckled. "Of course you are. Solo Stockton, that's what they are calling you."

"Yes, and I can live with that. I have heard worse."

"So, enlighten me, what fell into your lap?"

"You saw the woman that just left? She was dating the guy and she just turned over a lot of information that's going to help me nail Holden Griggs. Keep that between us."

"Is it information that should be shared with the FBI? You are aware that anything discovered on this guy is to be turned over right away," said Roland with concern.

"It will get to them. After I have checked it all out," Grant bragged. "I am, however, worried about her."

"Want me to keep an eye on her? Send me her address," Roland said, pulling out his phone.

"She refused help."

"That's never stopped us before."

"Before has never been this big. She thinks she will be in more danger if he expects that anyone is keeping an eye on her other than

his men. She could be right. She took a big risk coming here."

"Okay, if you change your mind, just say the word and I'm there. No one will notice me."

"Oh yes they will. Enjoy your poker thing and don't lose all of your money, you still owe me drinks for covering your ass on the last poker game that you lost miserably."

Roland laughed. "I got this," he said as he walked away.

# # #

"I should have insisted on protection for her. I should have made sure that she was on that plane," Grant said with remorse.

"And you think Holden either killed her or had her killed? To look like suicide," Park confirmed.

"That is what I believe," Grant answered. "And right now, he thinks that we have ruled her death a suicide and he's free."

"Oh?"

"This meeting is tonight and I'm planning on being there," Grant revealed.

"With back up I assume," Park suggested.

"I haven't told anyone else about this," Grant stated.

"So why are you telling me?" Park questioned.

"I'm not competing with you," he said with a smile. "I'm trusting that you will keep what I told you to yourself."

"I could always come with you tonight."

Grant chuckled. "I'm good Park."

"Holden isn't anyone to play around with," said Park. "You know that."

"I think I know that better than anyone as to how dangerous he is," he responded. "I'm only going to check it out and gather information. I need to know what he's up to and where he is operating. I have to get a step ahead of him."

Grant stood and walked to the door.

"I guess that's my cue," said Park, standing from his chair.

"It was good to see you again Park, but you do look a bit under the weather, are you alright?"

"If I had a dime for every time I was asked that," responded Park. "I'm okay. Just trying to figure things out."

"I'm still serious about getting that drink soon. Hopefully, you'll go and get some rest. Take care of yourself."

"Right," said Park. "Be careful out there."

# # #

There were twenty-five students in Sydney's history class listening to their teacher, Miss Harlow's lecture. A boy sitting next to Sydney passed her a note with a wink. Sydney sighed, took the note, and read it which suddenly caught the teacher's attention.

"Sydney, I hope that you are listening. You are all having a quiz tomorrow," Miss Harlow advised.

"I was listening until Jayden gave me this note," Sydney said, standing. "Anyone want to hear what it says?"

The class became noisy, all finding entertainment in what Sydney was doing to the boy who was visually embarrassed. He pleaded with his eyes to Sydney for her not to read what he had written. Miss Harlow approached and snatched the note from her.

"Not here Sydney. You're being very disrespectful," she said in disgust.

The teacher crumpled the note and tossed it in her trash can as she reached her desk. Sydney gave a sneer to

Jayden whose cheeks were turning red.

"Sit down Sydney," ordered Miss Harlow.

Sydney looked at Jayden as he rested his arms on his desk and buried his head.

"And to answer your question Jayden, no, I don't want to get pizza with you after school," she said in spite. "But thanks for thinking that my hair is absolutely gorgeous. I try."

The class began to chuckle as Jayden kept his head down. Miss Harlow became annoyed.

"Sydney, head on over to detention," she calmly said. "Now, please. And Jayden, you go too. You know the rules about causing distraction in class."

"Gladly," said Sydney, giving a cocky smile as she walked out.

She waited outside the classroom at the door until Jayden stormed out.

"Thanks a lot, Sydney," Jayden barked. "I can't believe you did that."

"And I can't believe you would think I'd ever waste my time dating someone as pathetic as you are. Why are you even in this school?"

Jayden ignored her and began walking down the empty hallway. Sydney went along behind him.

"Answer me Jayden!" she yelled. "Don't walk away from me! You're weak and there's no room for you here. You are such an embarrassment!"

Jayden was angry. He stopped walking and shoved Sydney who immediately became furious. She was about to lunge at him, but with the noise, several teachers including Miss Harlow, stepped out of their classrooms and into the hallway to find out what was happening. Before anyone could reach them, Sydney grabbed Jayden's hand and broke two of his fingers. She pushed him and walked calmly away.

"Sydney! Come back here!" shouted Miss Harlow. "If you walk away, you'll be not just suspended, but you'll be kicked out of this school!"

Sydney suddenly stopped walking. She raised her arms as if she were taking commands from a police officer and slowly turned around.

"Fine," she softly said. "It was self-defense. You have cameras all over the place. Just look, check out the video. He shoved me. He pushed me first."

Sydney watched with a grin at Jayden who was moaning in pain. Students peeked out of their classroom doors at the commotion.

Miss Harlow walked to Sydney who slowly put her hands down.

"Let's go," she said, gesturing for Sydney to walk to the principal's office.

As she walked with Miss Harlow, Sydney looked back to see other teachers helping Jayden.

"You may have broken his whole hand Sydney. Why would you do that?" she asked. "Was it worth it? Jayden is one of our best all-around sports players, you may have ruined his entire year."

A smirk appeared on Sydney's face as she continued walking with Miss Harlow, taking pleasure in what she did.

CHAPTER SIX

The fall season brought darkness to the early evenings. Grant sat in his car, out of sight in an abandoned industrial park across from where Holden was expected to be. He observed the trash trapped between the links of a fence that surrounded the building and the small traces of grass that were dry and brown. He felt anxious but kept reminding himself that he was only there to observe and to gather as much information as he could.

Forty-five minutes passed, Grant continued to stay alert, periodically looking through his binoculars for a better view. Suddenly, he saw car headlights from across the street and noticed two black four-door luxury sedans stopping at one of the abandoned buildings. Holden Griggs stepped out of the driver's side of the first car, leaving it running with the lights on. Holden was a large man in his late fifties. His skin was light brown and appeared to be a mixture of many ethnicities. He was dressed in casual but tailored attire and had an intimidating demeanor that matched his raspy and frightful voice.

Two men exited the second car, one a great deal larger and older than the other. Grant peered through his binoculars immediately recognizing Holden, but not able to identify the other two men. The older man carried no expression on his face. He had the look of a nightclub bouncer and was there to deliver the scrawny younger man who stood fearful as he fidgeted with his fingers. He shoved the thin man towards Holden who waited in front of his car. Once the young man faced Holden, the other man walked back to his car and drove away.

Grant watched as Holden gave the young man a few shoves away from the car until he was pushed against the wall of a building. The headlights of Holden's car gave Grant the view he needed to see what was going on. The conversation appeared to become heated as the young man began using hand gestures while he explained something. Holden stepped closer, yelling at the man until he dropped to his knees. Grant feared the worst and quietly exited his car. He jogged across the street with his gun drawn towards the side of the building where the men were.

Grant crept closer and closer, hiding around the corner, quickly and frequently glancing until he saw Holden pull a gun from the back of his pants and point it at the man's head.

"Please Mr. Griggs. I swear it was an accident! I didn't mean to lose it!" begged the man as he raised his quivering hands.

"Sorry isn't enough," said Holden in an angry tone. "For all I know, you took it for yourself. Are you selling my product on the side?"

"No, no! I'm not selling anything. I only deliver for you, Mr. Griggs. I swear to you!"

"I cannot trust you. You're a liability at this point and I cannot afford for my product to miss shipments."

Grant knew that he couldn't let Holden shoot the man. He sprung from around the corner of the building and into Holden's sight.

"Holden! Drop the gun!" he shouted, "You don't want to do this!"

Startled by Grant's order, Holden immediately aimed his gun at Grant, but he was not fast enough to pull the trigger. Grant had already shot a bullet into his chest. Holden's eyes bulged in shock and disbelief as he held his hand over his chest before falling to the ground.

"Don't move!" Grant shouted to the young man who was still on his knees with his trembling hands above his head.

Grant hurried to Holden who was lifeless. He kicked Holden's gun away from him and checked for a pulse, there was none. The young man that Holden was about to kill began to run in fear, and out of nowhere, Park appeared and tackled him. He pressed his face to the ground.

"Toss me your cuffs," Park yelled to Grant out of breath.

Grant was furious. He stormed to Park, shoved him off the man, and placed cuffs on him. Park immediately stood and ran to Holden's body.

"What are you doing!" Grant scolded.

"I gotta see his hands," Park mumbled.

Park desperately grabbed Holden's hands and examined them, hoping to see the marks. There were none. He checked both hands again just to be sure.

"Damn it! It's not him!"

While Grant was preoccupied with the young man. Park found the chance to quickly search Holden's pockets. He wasn't sure what he was looking for, but he was desperate to find anything. He found an envelope in his back pocket and shoved it in his jacket before Grant noticed. Grant pulled the frightened man up and pushed him against Holden's car.

"Don't move," he ordered before turning his attention to Park. "Park! What the hell are you doing here? Did you follow me?"

Park appeared crazed as he brushed his hands through his oily hair. "Yea, I did. I needed to know."

"Know what?" asked Grant.

Park suddenly focused on the young man and charged at him, pulling the man to him. He checked his cuffed hands that were behind his back. Nothing. No bars.

"Doesn't matter," Park said, panting and wiping his hand across his face.

"Are you crazy?" Grant shouted.

"Maybe I am, sorry man," he said in a defeated tone, walking away.

Grant watched in confusion as Park moved quickly out of sight. Grant turned back to the young man who stood in shock still leaning against the car.

"What was going on with you and Holden? Why did that man want to kill you?" Grant asked, pointing to the dead man. "Were you dipping into his profit or something?"

The young man was silent.

"Sit on your ass!" he ordered.

The man quickly sat on his bottom while Grant called for help. After he disconnected his call, he approached Holden's dead body and began searching his pockets. He pulled out his phone and a few receipts but nothing of importance. He then looked at both of Holden's hands.

He softly said with suspicion, "What the hell were you

looking for, Park?"

Grant marched back to the man.

"What about the guy that tackled you. You know him?" he asked as the sounds of sirens became louder.

The man wiped the sweat from the side of his face with his shoulder and said, "No, never saw him before."

Grant stood confused about Park, his eerie behavior, and his obsession with Holden.

# # #

It was routine for Sydney and Aubrie along with the other kids to gather in the living room to watch a television show before going to bed. That night's show was interrupted by a special news broadcast. They listened intently.

"Michigan's alleged drug trafficker, 58-year-old Holden Griggs, was shot and killed earlier tonight when he was spotted in the industrial district near downtown, holding a gun to another man's head. Detective Grant Stockton saw the young man in trouble and when Holden pointed his firearm at the detective, Stockton fired, shooting Griggs in his chest. He was pronounced dead at the scene. Griggs had been under FBI investigation for several months."

"Oh wow, that guy finally got caught. Didn't think that would ever happen," said a boy leaning on the back of a couch. "Glad I got my stash."

Aubrie periodically glanced across the room at Sydney who sat in a chair with a blank stare on her face. She wondered how long she was going to sit in that manner and why the broadcast affected her.

"What's up Sydney? You look like you lost your lover," teased the boy, getting chuckles from the other kids.

Sydney glared at him, stood, and without a word, walked up to her room. Aubrie came in and closed the door behind her. Sydney sat at their desk and began scribbling on a piece of paper with a pencil.

"I wish you would talk to me."

"I'm fine!" she snapped. "Just leave me alone!"

"Something's happened to you!" Aubrie cried.

"What are you talking about?" Sydney questioned in a disgusted tone.

Aubrie leaned against the door and crossed her arms.

"You've been acting strange ever since that lady gave you that doll. Where is it? I want to see it."

Sydney ignored Aubrie and continued scribbling on her paper. Aubrie stepped closer to her.

"Where's that doll?"

"Why do you care?" Sydney asked in a cold tone.

"You're a totally different person and those marks, they are getting darker and darker, and don't tell me you're just continuously coloring it with a black permanent marker."

Sydney dropped her pencil on her desk and sneered at her.

"I don't care if you believe me or not. Maybe we're not as close of friends as I thought we were. I'd never call you a liar."

"I'm not... I didn't call you a..." she said feeling intimidated. "I just don't understand."

"Stop interrogating me!"

Aubrie became angry. "I've been trying to be nice to you because you're my best friend and I want to help you. I'm not the enemy! Is it something I did?" Aubrie asked.

"Just leave me alone."

"Why did you look so weird when the news came on about that guy getting killed?"

"I wasn't looking any type of way Aubrie!" Sydney yelled. "Please, leave it alone."

Aubrie sighed. "I'm here when you want to tell me what is happening with you."

Sydney stood and walked to her bed. She inhaled deeply and plopped down. "I am going to go to sleep. It's a school night," she said with sarcasm and a smile that left Aubrie perplexed.

# # #

"Gotta love the mornings," said Park with humor as he slowly approached Milo in the parking lot outside the police station.

He was wearing the clothes he had on the previous night. It was close to eight o'clock. Milo had just arrived and was pulling his backpack and coffee from his car. He peeked over the hood of the car at Park.

"You're still looking rough. Long night out?"

Park opened the passenger door and hopped in. Milo raised an eyebrow and looked inside at him.

"We need to talk," Park said, looking over his sunglasses.

Milo sighed. He tossed his bag over his seat, placed his coffee back in the cup holder, and got in.

"Where to?" said Milo, shutting the door.

"How about the cafe a couple of blocks over?" suggested Park, leaning back in his seat and closing his eyes.

Milo could clearly see Park's declining health and was worried. He periodically glanced at him until he saw that he had fallen asleep. When they reached the cafe, Milo gave Park a shove to wake him.

"We're here. I probably should have let you sleep. I'm thinking this is the most you've closed your eyes since you went on leave," said Milo, stepping out of the car.

Park and Milo walked into the near empty cafe. They both plopped in comfortable chairs in a corner at the rear of the building.

"So, where did you go? You didn't answer my calls. I even stopped at your house and nothing."

Park pulled out the envelope that he snatched from Holden's jacket and held it in his hand.

"Grant went on surveillance to check out a lead he had on Holden Griggs," Park said. "I followed him."

"So, you were there when Holden was killed? Did Grant see you?" Milo asked with a look of surprise.

"I was, and yes, he did. Holden was about to kill this kid when Grant shot him. The kid took off and I stopped him. While Grant was dealing with the kid, I checked Holden's hands, for the marks. There weren't any, it's not him. Back to square one," he said, holding up the envelope. "Then I read this. Someone else wasn't happy with Sara, and the person that wrote this letter could very well be the carrier."

"Oh?" said Milo in curiosity. "Who is it from?"

"A girl, her name is Sydney," he said, handing the envelope to Milo. "At least that's what is on the envelope. No last name, no address, just Sydney."

Milo pulled the handwritten letter from the envelope and began to read.

"Holden has a kid?" questioned Milo. "She seems upset. She doesn't say Sara's name but..."

"We know who she's talking about," Park added. "The postmark on the envelope is the day before Sara's body was found."

Park reached and grabbed the letter from Milo.

He began to read, "Dad, I'm sorry that it did not work out with her. I know how excited you were about her being the one and how bad you wanted me to meet her, but I am happy that you found out early that she would never have your back. If she loved you, she would have agreed to stay by your side, not tell you that she's going back to Spain. I hate her for not giving you a chance."

Park paused, looked at Milo, and continued reading, "Speaking of hate, this camp is horrible. I have been here for close to a month, but I guess it is better than jail. But I'm not looking forward to going back to my foster home, it's horrible. At least I am still able to write to you and I hope one day soon it will be safe for me to come and live with you.'"

Park folded the letter and put it back in the envelope.

"We need to find her," he said.

"I am assuming that you took evidence off of Holden's body," Milo stated.

Park smiled. "Did I tell you I got this off his body?"

"Nope, guess you didn't," he replied.

"We know she's in a foster home and she must have done something pretty bad to have to go to luckily the only rehabilitation camp for juveniles out here," Park anxiously said, standing. "Piece of cake."

As the server approached, Milo looked up at Park and gestured for him to sit back down. Park chuckled.

"You're getting way ahead of yourself. I'm starving and you need to eat too," Milo said. "On me, order what you want. When we're done, I'll check to see if she's in the system which I'm guessing she will be. You're still on leave so please let me handle this. As soon as I find her, we'll pay her a visit."

Park sat and began reading the menu as the server approached.

# # #

After the two finished breakfast, Park went home and immediately began his search for the girl. He was too anxious to wait for Milo and before he knew it, hours had passed and he found himself sitting in his car staring across the street at an old house in Cliff County. The siding needed repair along with the cracked cement on the stairs that led to the door. The loose wood on the porch floor appeared to be a safety hazard.

He rubbed his temples hoping that the pounding in his head would go away. He also hoped that when his pursuit ended, the pain that was becoming more prevalent would end too. It had clearly taken a toll on his body.

Park didn't feel guilty about taking the letter from Holden's dead body, he needed to find and exhaust any lead he had to find the carrier.

He stepped out of his car and peered at the house for a moment longer before walking to the door and knocking. He looked down at a photo that he had of a young woman that he didn't even know, but it suited his purpose. He took a deep breath and exhaled before Joan opened the door wearing workout gear and wiping the sweat from her face with a towel.

"What can I do for you?" she asked through the screen door, throwing the towel over her shoulder.

Park pulled out his badge and revealed it to her. "I'm Detective Park Saire," he said, showing the photo of the girl to her.

"We are looking for this girl, she's a sixteen-year-old runaway. We received a tip that she was in this area and we're going door to door hoping someone has seen her."

Joan unlocked and opened the screen door and gestured for Park to enter. Park glanced around the dark and gloomy living room. Joan took the photo from him and examined it.

"No, I haven't seen her. Maybe one of my kids have," she said, turning to the stairs and calling. "Kids! Come down please."

"We'll be down in a minute," shouted a voice from upstairs.

Joan rolled her eyes with an embarrassed chuckle and said, "A minute means about five."

"It's fine. I appreciate your allowing them to look at the missing girl's picture," Park replied, looking at a wall covered with framed photos of several children varying in age.

"That is a lot of kids," he commented, trying to make small talk. "Do you foster children?"

"For twenty-two years now," she proudly answered. "My husband and I felt it was our calling. He died two years ago, but I know he would have wanted me to continue to help as many troubled kids as I could."

"Sorry for your loss," he said with sympathy.

"Thank you, please make yourself comfortable. Can I get you something to drink?" she asked, leading him to the sofa. "I have my own two children and I foster two twelve-year-old boys and two sixteen-year-old girls. The girls are quite the handful."

"Oh? How long have you had the girls?" he asked, sitting on the sofa. "At that age, I can imagine what you're going through."

Joan sat in a chair across from him. "About six months. An awfully long six months," she replied with a chuckle, shaking her head. "Sydney and Aubrie, they are inseparable and if trouble isn't following them, they are looking for it. I take in the kids that no one else can handle. Those two used a lot of intimidating tactics against their previous foster parents which is why they are with me."

"Thank goodness for people such as yourself that are willing to go that extra mile to help put them on the right path."

"Both just returned from a month at the juvenile rehabilitation camp up north. I'm hoping that it gave them a preview of what to expect in a detention facility which is much much worse."

"That's a serious camp. What did they do to get sent there?" Park asked.

"They hotwired a car with some older men, and then took it to a store that they attempted to rob. They, especially Sydney, seem to be magnets for attracting the wrong crowd," Joan explained.

Park raised an eyebrow. "You certainly do have your hands full."

"Yup," she commented as two of the younger kids hurried down the stairs followed by Aubrie and Sydney who took their time coming down.

Joan and Park stood to greet the kids.

"Kids, this is Detective Saire, he's looking for a girl who has run away," she announced, handing the picture to the kids who each passed it to the other shaking their heads.

"No," said Aubrie, handing the photo to Sydney. "I haven't seen her."

When Sydney reached for the picture, Park's eyes immediately froze on her right hand bearing the familiar bars. He could hardly believe that the person carrying the blood of Ostar was standing right in front of him. He hoped that his reaction and the long gaze was not suspicious. He was frozen as his mind took him once again back to that horrible night when Riley completed her part of Ostar's quest. He finally snapped back to reality when his heart began to race, pounding as if it were about to jump out of his chest. He thought he was going to hyperventilate and knew he needed to get out of the house.

"Nope, I haven't seen her either," Sydney commented, handing the photo back to him.

"Can we go now?" Aubrie asked.

Joan nodded and gestured for the kids to leave, which they were happy to do.

"I'm sorry Detective. I do hope you find her."

"Thank you," he said, fumbling to get the screen door open. "I have confidence that we will."

CHAPTER SEVEN

Park didn't know what to do with himself nor did he know what he was going to do now that he found the carrier of the curse. He paced in his living room for several minutes before he roamed into his dining room. He stood in front of the pictures of Ostar's victims, glancing at each photo before moving into the kitchen.

He grabbed the last bottle of water from the refrigerator, scooped the bottle of pills from the counter, and headed to the patio. He took a couple of pills and washed them down with water. His nerves had gotten the best of him and he could feel his heart pounding up to his head.

"Park!" Milo yelled in panic, swinging the front door open. "Where are you!"

"Out back," Park called, anxious when he heard his voice.

Milo walked briskly through the house and to the back patio to see Park pacing, almost in a frenzy.

"What's going on?" Milo asked as he suddenly slowed

his pace. "Your message scared me."

"Milo, it's her," Park whispered, rubbing his hands through his hair.

"It's who?" Milo asked, taking hold of Park's arm and guiding him to sit in one of the patio chairs. "Are you okay?"

"The daughter. Holden's daughter, Sydney. I saw her," Park said, rubbing his temples.

"I just got information on this kid. Why didn't you tell me that you found her?" Milo asked, annoyed. "What happened when you met her?"

"I couldn't wait and I didn't want to waste your time in case it was a dead-end, but it's her. She has the mark, she's the host. No doubt," he blurted as he applied more pressure to his temples with his fingers. "What information did you find on her?"

"She was taken away from her mother when she was five. The poor kid was addicted to drugs out the gate, she was in bad shape. Probably the best thing that ever happened was for her to be taken away. The mother died shortly after and there was no information on who the father was."

"And he managed to keep tabs on her all this time, it's remarkable," Park added. "I have been following suicide cases since Riley passed the curse, and I think that Sara was Sydney's first victim."

"Now that we know, what's next?" Milo asked.

Park quickly stood in anger pushing the chair over. "I don't know Milo! All I know is that I cannot let this happen again! I can't!"

"Calm down!" Milo ordered, standing, and picking up the chair. "Please, you gotta get a hold of yourself. Just take a deep breath and sit."

Park closed his eyes, took a couple of deep breaths,

and rubbed his temples again. He then sat back in the chair.

"You're starting to worry me, have you looked at yourself in the mirror? You're dwindling to nothing and all of this is making you nuts. You can't keep ignoring those headaches," Milo lectured. "You're falling apart."

"I'm fine. It's just stress," Park replied. "You don't need to be concerned about me, I'll be..."

Park suddenly began to think and sprang from his chair again.

"What?" questioned Milo. "What's wrong?"

"We need to get to Grant. He killed Sydney's father. He's going to be next," Park urged. "Come on!"

Milo walked with Park outside. He watched Park fumble for his keys with shaking hands.

"I'll drive," said Milo, rushing to his car with Park and hopping in.

"Do you know where he lives?" Milo asked as he began to back out of Park's driveway.

Park yanked Grant's card from his wallet and dialed his number, he listened for a moment and then disconnected the call.

"He's not answering at the station," he anxiously said, dialing another number and disconnecting the call again. "Damn it! It went to voice mail. I have no idea where he lives, just head out, we'll figure something out on the drive. It's gonna take over an hour to get there. This is not good."

Milo stopped the car before they were in the street. He picked up his cell phone and dialed a number.

"Mandie hey, this is Milo. I need a favor. Grant Stockton, he is a detective in Cliff County. I'm looking for his address. I wouldn't ask you if it wasn't extremely important."

Milo glanced at Park who looked like an addict starting to go through withdrawals. He was agitated and looked around as if he were paranoid.

"Thanks, text me the address. I owe you," said Milo as he disconnected the call and opened his text.

Milo pulled out of the driveway. He turned on the siren and sped to Grant's house hoping that they could make the seventy-mile journey quickly. They arrived with a screech into the driveway, exited the car, and rushed to the front door, both with a hand positioned on their guns. Park rang the doorbell and after only a second, he began pounding on the door.

"Grant! Grant! It's Park and Milo. Are you there?" shouted Park.

Milo grabbed Park's hand to stop him from beating on the door. Grant finally opened it.

"What in the world are you two doing here?" Grant asked, standing in the doorway in anger.

Park gave a sigh of relief and leaned against the frame of the doorway. "Thank God," he said.

"What the hell is going on?"

"Grant, may we come in?" Milo asked. "Please."

"We think your life may be in danger," Park added out of desperation.

Grant glared at the two for a moment before finally stepping back and gesturing for them to enter.

"Wanna tell me what's going on?" Grant asked, shutting the door and placing his hands on his hips before noticing Park's appearance. "Are you okay?"

"Grant," said Park, approaching him. "Your life is in danger."

Grant chuckled and stepped away from Park. "Aren't our lives always in danger?"

"He's serious man," Milo confirmed.

"The person that killed Sara is coming after you," said Park.

"I highly doubt that. The person that killed her is dead," Grant laughed.

"Okay, then believe this. There's someone out there that isn't happy that Holden is dead, and that person is coming for revenge," Park sternly said.

Grant chuckled again. "I'm sure there are a lot of unhappy people over Holden's death, but I don't think his men would risk bringing a firestorm of law enforcement on them for killing a cop."

"Grant, you gotta listen," Milo calmly said. "He's right."

"I don't have to listen to him or you. As you see, I'm fine and I'm going to stay that way," Grant said, walking to the door and opening it.

Both Park and Milo stared at Grant without moving.

Grant looked at Milo and said, "Take him to a doctor. He's not well."

Grant puffed his chest and placed his hands on his hips.

"I need both of you to leave," he ordered. "Now."

Milo sighed and hunched his shoulders before walking out of the house ahead of Park who stood paralyzed.

"Grant, please. I know you think that you found the person that took Sara's life, but you are wrong. You're wrong and you need to listen to me and believe me when I tell you that you are in danger. Holden didn't kill her."

Park's eyes were wide with determination. Grant stepped closer to him, studying his face.

"What were you looking for on Holden's body? Why were you so fixated on his hands?"

Park said nothing and continued looking into Grant's eyes. Grant looked over his shoulder to Milo who was standing outside the door.

"Milo, please come get your partner."

There was a moment of silence as Park turned and then suddenly glanced back at Grant, wishing that he would hear him out. Milo walked to Park and gave a quick tug on his shirt.

"Let's go, Park, he doesn't want to listen," said Milo.

Park stepped backwards out of the door. Milo grabbed his arm to continue moving him further from the door as Grant watched in anger.

"You need to get some help man," he loudly announced to Park.

"Sydney," he said, breathing hard.

"What?" Grant asked, still standing in the doorway.

"Her name is Sydney and she is coming for you," Park ranted like a crazed man.

"Come on Park. We need to leave," Milo urged.

Park threw his hands up. He walked to Milo's car in anger and hopped in.

"He's next, we can't just leave," he anxiously said as Milo got in the driver's side.

"What the hell are we supposed to do? We warned him and we better hope he doesn't call our captain, if he does, we're toast!"

"I don't know what to do," said Park, staring at the house. "She's going to be strong. Stronger than you can ever imagine. I don't have a plan, Milo. If she were to show up right now, I'd have no idea how to stop her. I couldn't stop Riley and I can't stop Sydney."

"She doesn't know where he lives," said Milo, hoping it would calm Park down.

Park closed his eyes fighting the pain that shot through his head. It did not last long, but the short stabs were so intense that he would lose his focus.

"She knows, trust me."

Milo sighed. "I'm going to act like that didn't just happen even though you've been wincing in pain ever since I got to your house. Am I going to have to drag you in to see a doctor?"

"We stop the deaths and I'll see a doctor. Deal?"

"Fine, so what are we going to do, just sit outside his house? And if she does come, how do we fight her?"

"It's not going to be easy and I don't even know how to succeed, but we gotta try and hope we don't wind up under her spell," Park explained in a defeated tone. "Even if we get the pen, I still don't know how to get it open."

"Open?"

"We learned from Frank that human blood mixed with Ostar's blood in the pen could stop the carrier and kill the curse. We got the pen from Riley for a moment, but there was no way to get the pen open."

"That is good to know, but if the pen won't open, what is next?" Milo asked, slowly articulating each word.

"You and I are going to visit her best friend at her high school in the morning and pray that Grant stays alive."

Milo sighed and said, "I think we are going to be spending a lot of time out here in Cliff County."

# # #

"How are you feeling?" Aubrie asked Sydney as they began their mile walk to school.

"I'm fine, why would you even ask me that?" Sydney quickly answered, adjusting her backpack over her shoulders.

Sydney suddenly stopped walking. Aubrie took a few more steps before realizing that Sydney was not next to her. She stopped and turned to see Sydney walking the other way.

"Syd!" Aubrie shouted as she ran to catch her. "Where are you going?"

Sydney gently placed her hands on the sides of Aubrie's face and looked sincerely into her eyes.

"There's something I have to do," said Sydney with a straight face.

"What do you have to do?" Aubrie suspiciously asked. "We can't be late for school. You know that."

"You're not going to be late, please go. I'm going to be a little late. I'll be there by third period," she said with a smile.

She turned and walked in the opposite direction. Aubrie watched her for a moment before she began her walk to school alone.

Until recently, Aubrie looked up to Sydney. She shadowed her every thought and action and found it normal to never react or make a move without Sydney going first. She had a way of getting her to do what she wanted. She was a risk-taker and never thought or cared about the consequences of anything that she did. Even though Aubrie knew that the things Sydney did were wrong, she envied her confidence and lack of fear.

Aubrie did not know if she had any blood relatives or if they just didn't want to come forward to take her in. All she knew was that no one ever showed up to claim her, which left her subject to bitterness every time she was placed in a new home. Although Aubrie looked forward to a better future with hopes to even go to college, she was broken along with the other foster children that were around her. She also knew that if she were to free herself from the glimpse of a dreaded future behind bars, she would have to either free herself from Sydney or somehow hope that the consequences that seemed to be a pattern for them would open Sydney's eyes. Aubrie wanted Sydney to think more like her because she desperately needed to change the course of her dismal life and it was up to her to make that happen.

She turned back and saw nothing. Sydney was gone.

# # #

As soon as Sydney had enough distance from Aubrie and knew she was out of sight, she sprinted away reaching her ten-mile destination in only a few minutes.

Sydney was in a middle-class neighborhood where the streets were wide and the homes were spacious. The houses were older, but all were well kept showing the neighborhood's pride of ownership. There was only one house that she was interested in and she stood directly in front of it for several minutes as if she were in a trance. She finally stepped to the door and knocked.

The door opened, it was Grant.

"Can I help you?" he asked as he put on his suit jacket. "I'm not interested in buying whatever you're selling and I'm just getting ready to leave."

Sydney's demeanor changed to that of a frightened and timid girl.

"There's a car with a couple of guys in it that are chasing me. I ran to two other homes and no one would answer. Please help me!" she cried.

Grant poked his head out of the door and looked over Sydney in both directions.

"Step inside," he said, guiding her in.

Sydney quickly walked into the house.

"Can you describe the men in the car and what kind of car they were in?" he asked as he shut the door and turned to her. "What's your name?"

"It's Sydney," she said with fury.

Grant's eyes widened, recalling the last thing Park said to him as Milo dragged him from his home. He tried to grab the gun from his holster, but the whites of Sydney's eyes had already turned to blood. She leaped on him, digging her thumbnail into his cheek. He immediately went into a daze, looking at her as if he were silently taking her directions. He walked into the kitchen, opened the door that led to the garage, and stepped out with Sydney following close behind. Her eyes were still filled with blood.

Grant lifted a gas can that was half full and snatched a lighter that sat on a counter. He stumbled past her and back into the house only to walk out of the front door. Sydney continued to follow him until she reached the door. She could see neighbors outside, some jogging, and others pulling trash bins to the curb. She closed the front door behind Grant and peered out the bay window making sure to stay out of sight.

A neighbor that lived across the street was at the corner of his yard pulling weeds when he saw Grant walk to the center of the street with the gas can.

"Hey Grant," the neighbor called. "What's going on? You run out of gas or something?"

Grant looked directly at his neighbor who had begun to take a few steps towards him.

"Grant? You okay?" the neighbor asked with suspicion.

Grant said nothing, he immediately lifted the can and poured the gas over himself.

"Grant! Stop!" yelled the man, running to him but halting when he saw Grant pull out the lighter.

In no time, Grant was engulfed in flames as people frantically ran to help. The neighbor quickly ran into his house and came back out with a fire extinguisher. He blasted Grant, but it was too late, he was already charred and dead, leaving those around him standing in shock.

Sydney still watched from inside the house as another neighbor ran to Grant's body with a blanket and threw it over him while another called for help. Sydney's eyes turned back to normal and with a grin, she strolled to the back of the house and out the patio door. She hopped a few fences with ease and headed to school feeling fully satisfied with what she had done.

# # #

Milo and Park arrived at Sydney and Aubrie's school. They stepped out of Park's car and began walking to the entrance.

"Exactly what are we doing here?" he asked. "This wasn't a quick trip around the block to get here."

"Her friend, Aubrie, she may be able to help. I met her yesterday with Sydney. The foster mom said that they are inseparable. She will have for sure noticed a change in her," he said, swiftly walking through the parking lot to the front door. "We need to find out what she knows."

Milo stopped walking as they were about to enter the building. "Sydney has this doll. You're sure of that right?"

"I told you that she had the marks on her hand, which means she has the doll and we are going to figure out how Aubrie can help us get it and the pen."

The two walked into the school and to the reception desk.

"Hi, is your principal available?" Park asked, showing his badge.

"Of course," said the receptionist who quickly lifted the phone and called for the principal.

Park and Milo stood patiently and silently as they waited momentarily.

"Can I help you?" asked the middle-aged woman, stepping out of her office. "I am Principal Warren."

"I'm Detective Saire and this is Detective Savatt. We are investigating an assault that happened in Fraiser County and we believe that one of your students was a witness to the incident. Her name is Aubrie Johnson," said Park, quickly glancing at Milo. "Is there a room where we can speak with her in private?"

The principal turned and said to the receptionist, "Would you please have Aubrie Johnson come to the office?"

She turned to the men.

"Aubrie is one of our students in foster care. We will need to call her foster mother," she advised.

Milo glanced at Park as the receptionist hung up the phone.

"No need, she is on her way. We'd appreciate it if you could have her join us when she arrives."

"Of course," said Principal Warren, giving a nod to the receptionist.

The receptionist looked up Aubrie's schedule, picked up the phone, and called her classroom. She softly spoke to request Aubrie and moments later, Aubrie walked into the office. The principal escorted her and the detectives to an empty classroom where Aubrie sat at a desk at the head of the classroom. Both Milo and Park leaned against the teacher's desk.

"Aubrie," said Park. "This is my partner, Detective Milo Savatt."

Aubrie innocently smiled at him as Park moved to a desk beside her and sat.

"I told you yesterday that I didn't know the girl in the picture."

"Yes, I know," said Park. "We need to talk to you

about your friend, Sydney."

"What about her?"

"Have you noticed a change in her? Anything at all."

"Like what?"

"Anything Aubrie. Any change in her emotionally, does she anger quickly. Has she stopped eating? Is she physically stronger?"

Aubrie looked at both men.

"All of it and how would you know this?" she blurted. "She's not the easiest person to get along with but now she is worse. She used to never get mad at me and lately, she's been treating me like she does everyone else. And yes, she is very strong. We were at this camp for a month and I'd never seen her or anyone for that matter do push-ups like she did. She could barely run a quarter of a mile here in gym class but out there, she ran a mile faster than anyone and wasn't even out of breath."

"When did you notice the change?" Milo asked.

"It's so weird. On our way to the camp, we stopped to get snacks at a little store and when we came out, there was a homeless lady. She asked us for change. I didn't have any, but Syd did, and she gave her a few quarters. Then the lady insisted on giving Syd this awful dirty and ugly doll. Syd took the doll and she's been different ever since," Aubrie said with emotion. "It means something, I know it."

"I am not trying to scare you but..." Park said with hesitation. "Your friend isn't the same and it's because of what was inside that doll that the homeless lady gave to her."

"What do you mean?" Aubrie questioned, listening carefully to Park.

Park looked up to Milo who was uneasy about her being told that there was a curse.

"You said that you noticed Sydney's behavior change after the homeless lady gave her a doll?"

The girl nodded.

"I saw marks on her hand yesterday when she handed me the photo. They resemble the first few lines of a giant bar code and those marks weren't there before she got the doll, correct?"

"Yes, she said she made the marks herself with a permanent marker. I don't even know how or where she would have gotten a marker at the camp," she responded. "She even took off without anyone seeing her and I have no idea how she was able to get out and back without getting caught. Whatever is going on has got to be pretty serious for detectives to be involved."

"There was a pen inside the doll and the ink in that pen is... is," Park tried to explain, looking once again at Milo who had crossed his arms. "It's like a bad drug. If it's absorbed in the skin, it makes the person do things they normally wouldn't do... harmful things to other people. We believe that the marks on her hand are from that pen. It's what is causing the changes in her. We need your help to get it."

Aubrie's eyes widened as she pushed her hair from her face. "So, it's a drug that someone made? Are you looking for the person that did this? Can't you just go in and take it?"

"We are looking for the person that made it," Milo quickly replied. "But, we can't just go and take it from Sydney."

"Why?" Aubrie asked with nervousness.

There was a moment of silence before Milo sighed.

"Aubrie, it's complicated. The person that is responsible is very powerful. We can't let Sydney know that we know she has the pen," said Park.

"What?" Aubrie shouted. "This doesn't make sense!"

"Calm down," said Park. "If this gets out, all it is going to do is create unnecessary panic and we're sorry that we have to ask you to do this. This is the closest we have ever gotten to being able to get that pen. We can't catch who is responsible without your help."

"Why aren't you telling this to Syd?"

"You've already told us that she's not herself which she isn't. We can't risk her running away," Milo added.

"Once we have that pen, we'll be able to learn more about it with hopes to find out who created it and how to reverse whatever this is. We'll be able to get Sydney the help that she needs," Park explained.

"It's just the one pen?" she asked.

"As far as we know, yes," Park replied.

"Syd has always been hard to get along with. She doesn't trust many people. But how she is acting now is not her. I just don't know how I am supposed to get it from her. We are together almost all the time," she explained and then hesitating. "Except for this morning."

"What do you mean?" Park asked.

"She was acting normal when we started walking to school but then, out of the blue, she tells me that she had something to do, which was weird and she ditched. She said she would be back by third period," said Aubrie. "Do you think this is that dangerous? Can't we take her to a doctor? Somehow get whatever is in her system, out?"

Park quickly stood and looked down at Aubrie in concern.

"You don't know where she went?" he asked, ignoring her question.

"I don't but she was pretty determined to go. Joan's not going to be happy when she finds out."

"Listen, we need to go," Park said with urgency,

pulling a card from his wallet and handing it to her. "Do you have a phone?"

Aubrie nodded. Park slid his phone from the back pocket of his jeans and gave it to her.

"Please, put in your number. Just be careful around her."

"You're scaring me," said Aubrie as she put her number in his phone.

Her hands trembled as she handed the phone back to Park.

"That's not our intent, but this is serious," said Milo. "As long as she doesn't get extremely angry, you'll be okay."

"Okay, that makes me feel much better," she said with sarcasm.

"If you need anything, call. I'll send you a message on where and when to meet us with the doll," Park said, walking to the door and opening it.

Aubrie rushed to him in fear.

"Wait," she begged.

"You can do this," he said with encouragement. "We are going to do everything we can to get help for Sydney, but we can't do anything without the pen. It'll be inside that doll and when you see it, don't touch it. Right now, we must go. Everything is going to be okay and please don't say anything to anyone."

Park rushed out of the classroom with Milo following closely behind.

"What the hell Park," Milo complained. "What is going on?"

"She skipped class," he said in a jog through the corridor.

"Oh my God. Grant," was all Milo said as they made it outside and to the car.

Park and Milo left the school and raced to Grant's house with lights flashing and the siren blaring. The street where Grant lived was already blocked by police cars. They could see a fire truck and an ambulance closer to Grant's house.

"We're too late," said Park as they got out of his car and slowly walked towards the house.

# # #

Aubrie watched her third-period history teacher as he walked up and down the aisles in the classroom and finally back to the head of the class. Her head was so clouded from her conversation with Park and Milo that she couldn't hear any of the words that he spoke. All she could think about was what she had learned about the marks on Sydney's hands and the sudden rush for the men to leave when she announced that Sydney had skipped class.

She wondered where she went and if she would make it back before the end of class. The more the teacher paced around the class with his lecture, the more anxious she became. She couldn't stop herself from constantly looking over her shoulder at the door until it finally opened, and Sydney stepped in.

"I'm so sorry that I am late," she said to the teacher giving him a slip of paper. "My foster mom just dropped me off from my doctor's appointment. We didn't expect it to take as long as it did."

The teacher smiled. "It's okay Sydney, I hope you are feeling alright. Go take your seat."

Sydney gave an innocent smile and walked to her seat which was behind Aubrie. Aubrie turned and gave a suspicious glare. Sydney grinned at her before paying attention to the teacher.

When class was over, Sydney quickly scooted out of the classroom before Aubrie who bolted after her. She caught up to her and grasped her arm. Sydney snatched away.

"Stop it!" she snarled. "Don't touch me!"

"Where did you go?" Aubrie demanded in anger. "Did you forge a note to get into class? Joan would never sign a note to skip classes for any reason. Where did you go? You didn't have a doctor's appointment. I wanna know where you went."

Sydney ignored her and continued to walk with Aubrie following close behind her.

"Syd, wait!"

Sydney stopped and turned to her in anger.

"If you don't leave me alone, you're going to be sorry Aubrie."

"Are you threatening me?" Aubrie questioned with a frown on her face. "I can't believe you! Something is wrong with you and you need to talk to someone about it. I would have thought it would be me but I guess not. I'm done showing you that I care! You know we have to go to work tonight, are you planning on skipping that too and doing whatever you're doing? I swear I don't even know you anymore and I'm starting not to care!"

"Oh stop being such a whiny little bitch. It doesn't look good on you," Sydney sneered as she strolled away, leaving Aubrie confused.

CHAPTER EIGHT

Park was distraught over Grant's death. He found the carrier of the curse but had no idea of how to stop it. He felt sick with thoughts of what happened to the Rucker family weeks ago only for it to be happening again. He felt helpless. All he could do was follow the deaths until he could discover a way to kill Ostar. He laid on his bed looking at the ceiling, losing hope. His phone rang, it was Milo.

"Hey," he said in a depressing tone. "Oh? It's on the news?... Okay, sure. I could use the company. I'll see you here in about a half-hour."

Park ended the call and dragged himself to the living room. He grabbed the television remote and turned it on to see a news broadcast that revealed a headshot of Grant on the screen.

"Detective Grant Stockton died this morning from an apparent suicide," reported the journalist. "A neighbor caught this horrific incident on video which may not be suited for all viewers."

Park watched the video showing Grant in the middle of the street outside of his house pouring gasoline over his head. The image of his body was blurred the moment he lit himself on fire, and as his body burned, Park took note of how still Grant stood before he dropped to the ground. He snapped himself out of his paralyzed state of mind and rewound the video to just before the blaze of fire. He approached the television and studied the blank look on his face along with the cut on his cheek. He replayed it over and over until Milo arrived. He paused the screen on Grant's face.

"I wish he would have listened to us," Milo said with remorse.

"It doesn't matter, she would have got him no matter what," Park said in a defeated tone.

Milo sighed and said nothing as he turned his attention to the television. He glanced at Park who rewound and played the broadcast again, freezing it at the same spot to show Grant's face before it was blurred.

"You see that? The cut, it's the same as the others. And his face, no expression whatsoever."

"According to what this Frank guy told you about these carriers taking three souls, she's got one left," he said. "But you gotta listen to what I have to tell you."

Milo walked into the kitchen and stood at the small island.

"You also said that Frank was told by Ostar that he had to have 20 human souls every hundred years to bring life back to his realm, right?"

Park nodded as he walked in.

"I did some searching and I believe that I found the first host," he said. "I found a post, several recent posts from a man, his name is Thomas Etterly and he swears that his wife was cursed and that she was the cause of three deaths before she took her life."

Park's interest was more piqued. "How recent?"

"A little under three months ago. Then they stopped."

Park was speechless for a moment as he thought.

"His wife had the curse before Frank's daughter. If what Frank said is true then she has to be the first."

"I couldn't find any other strange connections involving suicides prior to that. I even searched surrounding states," Milo informed. "I made a few calls and I found out where Thomas Etterly is. He's at Highview."

"The psychiatric hospital?"

Milo nodded. "Which is why the posts stopped. Apparently, he was ranting and raving about this to the point that his daughter had him committed. I can't blame her, it's a hard pill to swallow," he said. "We can be there in two hours if you are up for a road trip."

Park grabbed his jacket, keys, and wallet. "I'll drive," he said as both rushed out of the door.

# # #

"Thomas hadn't had visitors since he was admitted and hasn't spoken a word," informed a female caretaker at Highview Psychiatric Hospital.

She escorted Milo and Park down the corridor of the facility to Thomas' room. She peeked inside to see him sitting in his usual spot, in a chair watching the news on the television with the remote gripped in his hand. Unless he was being escorted for meals into the cafeteria or in the lounge for activities, he would be in his chair in front of the television.

He was only sixty-two years old and never dreamed that he would be spending his days and nights inside a mental hospital. He didn't belong there, he said to himself over and over, yet he was trapped.

"Thomas," said the caretaker. "You have a couple of visitors."

Milo and Park stepped into the small room where the man sat peering at the television screen. He ignored them.

"Thomas," said the caretaker in a louder tone. "Would you like to have visitors?"

Park approached the man and whispered in his ear, "Thomas, does Ostar mean anything to you? Because if it does, we could use your help in stopping him."

It was as if a nerve was struck in Thomas' head. He snapped his attention to Park and then to the caretaker.

"Leave us," the man ordered the caretaker in a raspy tone. "And close the door."

The caretaker was surprised at the voice that she had never heard. "Let me know if you need anything," she said to Park and Milo before walking out and closing the door.

"Sit," he grumbled, pointing to his bed.

Park sat while Milo continued to stand.

"What do you know?" asked the man, scratching his head, then smoothing down his thin white hair.

"Thomas, we know that your talk about a curse landed you here," said Milo.

"Call me Tom, my friends call me Tom. These bitches here aren't my friends."

"But we don't even know you, we hardly could be your friends," Park chuckled.

"My friends and my believers," Tom said, giving a weak grin. "My daughter put me here. Wouldn't consider a word that I had to say. I guess she got her wish, her mother is gone, I'm here and she's off the hook to take care of either of us. Kids are ungrateful these days, all about themselves."

Tom leaned back in his chair. There was silence for a moment.

"Where did you hear the name Ostar? I have never mentioned that name. Which means I may have a chance with you. A chance to finally be heard and a chance that you believe what I say. If you know his name, it means you know that there is someone out there who carries a curse."

Park leaned closer to Tom.

"A young girl, her name was Riley Rucker, she found a doll. Inside the doll was a pen. The ink from the pen leaked on her hand and she changed, just like your wife, am I right? Then people started dying, by suicide and all connected to her. Somehow, they angered her," said Park. "And before Riley, there was a man named Frank. Ostar gave him the doll and it wound up in his daughter's hands. She hosted the curse that took my sister's life."

"Had I just spent more time looking for who carried this evil rather than spouting off thinking people would believe me, I could have been of help. After I was put here, all I did was watch the news. I heard about the suicides in Frasier County. That's it, just suicides and no one was looking into it. At least I thought. Which one was your sister? The bathtub or the jumper?"

Park became uneasy. He cleared his throat, clasping his hands together, and bowing his head. Milo sat beside him.

"She... She jumped off the top of the sorority house where she lived."

"I'm sorry for your loss," he said with sympathy. "We are all undoubtedly after the same thing. If you can get me out of here, I can help."

"Tom, you're definitely not insane," said Milo. "The problem is there's nothing we can do."

"Get me out of his shit shack!" Tom shouted.

"Calm down," instructed Park. "Milo's right, plus there's nothing you can physically do to help. Honestly, this may be the safest place for you. For now. The man who warned me of this curse reminds me of you."

"If he didn't also wind up in a hell hole like this, he's certainly smarter than I am," Tom grumbled.

"He didn't wind up in a place like this, but he's also dead and I'm not going to watch you die like I watched him," Park said, becoming emotional. "Help us by telling us everything that happened to your wife. Maybe there's something that could help us figure out what he really wants and how we can stop him."

"How did your wife get the doll?" Milo asked.

Tom sighed and leaned forward in his chair, finally able to tell his story without receiving doubt.

# # #

"Well, it's about time you came home," said Tom as he approached his wife, Penny, who had just stepped in the house from the garage carrying plastic bags filled with items that she purchased. "I was starting to think you bought out the entire swap meet."

Penny chuckled, putting the rest of the bags on the table. Inside one of them was a dirty doll made of material and stringy orange yarn for hair.

"Look what I got," she said, lifting the doll to him.

"Hope you didn't pay much for it," he replied.

Penny chuckled again. "It was free, the woman at the booth didn't know how it got on her table with the rest of what she was selling so, she said I could have it."

"Good thing. I'm surprised that she didn't pay you to take it," he laughed.

"Very funny. She just needs a bit of cleaning up. Maybe I'll make a new dress for her," she said. "On another note, I think I

am going to pass out early. This project for work with all the early hours is killing me. It doesn't help that Bobby plays his loud music and throws parties until the sun comes up. I hate living next door to that inconsiderate kid."

"Let's hope he wears himself out and it stops," Tom replied. "I'm sorry that he's keeping you up. Maybe try sleeping pills."

She looked at Tom and smiled. "This is what I get for marrying a man ten years older, you're retired and you can catch up on your sleep during the day."

"I can try talking to him again," Tom suggested.

"Don't you dare," she scolded. "We saw what happened last time you went to talk to him."

Tom chuckled and rubbed his hip. "It was just a bruise and I'm okay."

"He shoved you to the ground, Tom. He could have broken your hip. We're not young anymore. You should have pressed charges."

"He's a stupid entitled kid. He's got a lot of growing up to do."

"And his parents certainly aren't helping. They have only enabled him by giving him that house. I don't think he even has a job," Penny commented. "But, we just have to hope that we get a break tonight. I could certainly use the sleep."

Tom gave a wink and turned his attention back to the doll that Penny was still holding.

"What are you going to do with that ugly doll? Provided you can clean that thing up."

"First I am going to take this dirty dress off of it and..." she said as she discovered an opening in the back of the doll. "What's this?"

Tom watched Penny pull the back open and yank out a pen.

"What an odd-looking pen," he responded.

"Sure is and looks pretty old," she said as she examined it. "Maybe it's worth some money."

As Penny held the pen, ink slowly began to leak onto her hand.

"Guess not," she said with a chuckle, setting the doll and the

pen on the counter and running water on her hand under the faucet.

She scrubbed and scrubbed at the ink that had formed four bars on her hand, but it would not come off. Tom stepped in to help her.

"What the hell is it?"

"It won't come off!" she exclaimed as she suddenly stopped scrubbing and looked through the window above the sink. She gasped before looking at Tom, giving him a chance to see her pupils quickly flash, then disappear.

"Penny? Are you okay? Your eyes!"

Penny's demeanor changed from sweet to cold. "I'm fine," she sternly responded. "What's wrong with my eyes?"

"Are you sure you're okay, you're acting rather strange and your eyes flashed. At least I thought they flashed," Tom said in a suspicious tone.

"Oh, it was probably the glare from the sun," she quickly replied.

"Let me see your hand again. Maybe we should go to urgent care or the ER, there's no telling what this is."

Tom reached for her hand and she pulled away. She grabbed the pen, placed it back in the doll, and calmly walked away leaving him standing in confusion.

That night, Tom was not able to sleep. He found himself watching Penny and her erratic breathing, something she had never done before. He knew something was wrong and he was sure that it was because of the ink that had been absorbed in her skin. He stared at his wife until he finally fell asleep.

When he woke the next morning, Penny had already left for work. He was nervous the entire day waiting for her to come home. Finally, as the time reached close to six, Penny walked in acting like her normal self.

"How was your day?" he asked, somewhat relieved. "I was worried about you. Are you feeling okay?"

"My day was good. I'm feeling refreshed," she answered with no emotion. "I'm going to go change."

"Okay, and how about I make us a couple of chicken salads for dinner?"

Penny frowned and said, "Honestly, I'm not hungry, but go ahead and make something for yourself."

Tom watched her stroll down the hallway to the bedroom before walking to the front of the house and into the living room. He suddenly saw flashing lights through the window and went outside to investigate. He stood at the edge of his property watching and wondering what had happened as a gurney carrying a body was rolled out of the house next to his. He saw another neighbor, Doug, standing across the street also observing. He joined him.

"Hey Doug, what happened?"

"It looks like we won't be up all night anymore to the sounds of a bunch of drunks and loud music," Doug replied.

"What? What happened? Was that Bobby that they brought out?"

"Yep. He killed himself."

Tom was shocked. "Oh my God. How did you find that out?"

"I was outside when his parents showed up, they let themselves in and seconds later I hear this scream from the mom. I ran over and saw Bobby hanging. I called the police," Doug explained. "I guess his parents were picking him up to go on some sort of trip with them. It was awful. He tied a rope to the second-floor balcony and jumped. Guess we never truly know what's going on with people. He must have had been fighting some ugly demons."

"That is just terrible," Tom sadly said.

Doug pointed to the couple, both in their forties, standing in the doorway under the porch light with a policeman. They held tightly to one another sobbing.

"Those are his parents. Such a shame that someone that young felt that it was his only way out."

Doug turned and walked into his house leaving Tom alone watching the body being loaded into an ambulance. He sighed and walked back across the street and into his house. Penny was just coming out of the bedroom and into the kitchen, noticing the saddened look on Tom's face.

"What's wrong?" she asked.

"It's Bobby, next door."

"What about him?" Penny questioned in a bitter tone.

"You didn't notice the police cars, the ambulance in front of his house, and all the lights when you came in?"

"Did you?" she asked without a care.

"I've been at the back of the house all day, so no, I didn't notice until I went into the living room."

"What goes on over there is none of our business. That's what he repeatedly told us when we politely asked him to turn his music down," she remarked.

"He's dead Penny. He killed himself."

"No loss there," she quickly responded with no concern. "I need to run out and pick up my dry cleaning. I forgot to stop on my way home."

Penny grabbed her purse and walked out of the door that led to the garage.

Tom knew that Penny had ill feelings towards Bobby, but he was concerned with her lack of empathy. Bobby was rude, self-centered, and never cared about his neighbors no matter how much he disturbed them, but he never expected the reaction Penny had given.

# # #

"The second she came home from that swap meet with that doll, was when our lives changed for the worst. She went to the dry cleaners and was gone an incredible amount of time. When she finally made it home, I asked her what took her so long and she said that someone at the cleaners destroyed her blouse and she was at the mall looking for a new one," he explained. "I didn't give it much thought until I heard on the news that a woman who worked at that very same dry cleaners had committed suicide by ingesting some sort of cleaning solution right in front of the customers."

Milo and Park felt compassion for the man as they listened to his story. To anyone else, Tom sounded out of his mind, but to Park and Milo, he was the confirmation they needed to continue their quest.

"It couldn't be a coincidence, the neighbor and then the clerk at the dry cleaner, both who Penny had not only been in contact with but also gotten angry with. I can't say for sure that the woman that killed herself at the cleaners was the same woman that Penny was mad at but I know it in my gut. It was out of character for her to lose her temper with anyone. Sure, she complained about things like any other person and she would get annoyed, but overall, she wasn't an angry person. You would have thought the same if you knew her," he said, reaching for a glass of water that sat on a table beside his chair.

Tom was filled with so much anxiety that his hands trembled and he could not help spilling water in his lap. Milo took the glass from him and held it to his face. He sipped through a straw that was already in the glass.

"What happened next Tom?" Milo softly asked, placing the glass back on the table.

"She became a stranger overnight. I could barely see that she was my wife. She stopped eating and... and... at night, in her sleep, I would hear her softly call out the name," Tom said with a pause. "Ostar. I mean it was a whisper, but it was clear. I had to know what was going on. I wasn't even sure if she was still going to work, so, the next day I decided to follow her. Every morning she would drive to the station and take the train to work. That morning at the station, I saw her arguing with a man, I am not sure what it was about, but with how

Penny had been acting, it could have been anything. The man seemed to have gotten tired of arguing with her and walked around a corner. She did too and then returned with a crazed look on her face and... and her eyes, they were filled with blood."

Park and Milo watched as Tom wiped tears from his cheeks.

"Seconds later, the man appeared, moving like he was sleepwalking. He had this cut on his face and I saw him step willingly onto a train track seconds before the train arrived. After the man killed himself, I saw my wife happily take her life."

"How?" Park asked.

"She always carried a nail file. One of those silver pointy ones. She was obsessed with her nails being perfect. Never would I have imagined that it would be used to take her life. She stabbed herself in the neck. She went quickly."

"I'm sorry," said Milo, placing a hand on Tom's frail shoulder. "We believe you."

"Tom, can you tell us what happened to the doll before your wife took her life?" Park softly asked.

"She had it in her bag. She threw it and I saw where it went. It landed on top of one of the train cars about fifteen or twenty back. My wife was already gone, there was nothing that I could do for her, so I left her there to look for the doll. I knew it had done something to her and I could not let it get into the hands of anyone else so, I climbed up to the top of each car until I found it. I made sure that the pen was inside, and I took it home. I buried it in my back yard."

"Obviously it didn't stay there," Park commented. "Frank said that he met Ostar one night in the woods as he was about to legitimately take his life. Ostar offered him the doll and in return, he gave him a lot of money which he took for his family. Ostar somehow got the doll from your back yard and kept the cycle going by giving it to him."

"About a week later I went into my back yard, the ground was dug up and it was gone. How, I don't know," Tom replied.

"Did you or anyone ever touch the pen before it was buried?"

"A day before it went missing from my yard, my dog dug it up. She scratched at it until she somehow got the pen out. I came home and saw it on the ground. I carefully put it back in the doll. I knew that ink was the poison that changed my wife, so I made sure to not let it get on me. I dug a deeper hole and dropped it in. The next day, it was gone and there was no way my dog would have been able to dig it up that time," he explained. "What's his plan?"

"It's his realm, he supposedly needs twenty souls from our world to bring it back to life, but we can't be sure if that's even true," explained Park.

"Tom, did your wife say anything other than Ostar's name?"

"Before she died, she mumbled something. She said that starting with her, Ostar's journey had begun and those after her would be destined to become a part of his world," he softly said.

Park glanced at Milo. "Your wife Penny, then Lacey, Riley, and now Sydney. There is one more left. Sydney's going to have to pass it."

"I can't stay here," Tom said with anxiety. "Can you convince these people that I'm not crazy?"

Milo and Park glanced at one another and then to Tom.

"Tom," said Park, kneeling in front of him. "Right now, like we said, this is the best and safest place for you, but if you start telling them what they want to hear and screw the truth, you'll be out before you know it."

"Soon as we get past whatever this is, we promise we'll help get you out," Milo added.

"If you think of anything else that could help us, please call," Park said, giving Tom his card.

"Thank you both," Tom said. "Be safe and good luck."

CHAPTER NINE

"What do you think about the time between Tom's wife dying and Frank's daughter getting the doll?" Milo questioned, looking over the car at Park. "Ostar couldn't find it until Tom touched the pen after his dog dug it up. He reburies it and poof, next time he goes out, it's gone."

"He's blind until the pen is touched. The same thing happened when I was at the Rucker home with Riley. We can stop the cycle if we can just get the pen and never let it get into anyone else's hands," said Park, rubbing his temples and shutting his eyes tightly. "It's not a perfect fix by any means, but it's something."

"We better come up with a plan fast, for all we know, Sydney has already found her last soul."

"She's different," said Park. "We know she killed Sara and Grant but she's different than the other carriers."

"What do you mean?"

"Well," Park sighed. "It was a matter of days for the others to carry out their mission. Sydney has more control. She's had the curse for over a month. This thing seems to trigger when the carrier becomes enraged at someone. A wave of anger that exceeds their normal threshold so to say," Park explained. "Sydney's seems to be much higher."

"Which means for Sydney, it will take a lot to get her angrier than what she normally would," Milo suggested.

"It's one thing Ostar apparently didn't think of and it'll work in our favor. We have more time to make a plan and pray that Aubrie can deliver us that doll."

"And then what?" Milo asked.

"I don't know," Park replied in frustration. "Frank said that the blood from a non-sinner can stop someone that is being forced into taking their life. Like I said, Quinn saved her babysitter by dropping her blood into the cut that Riley put on her cheek. I don't know how or if it can work on a carrier, but we have to try. The pen isn't going to open, it won't break."

"So, if we can change Sydney's course, Ostar may show himself. And to do that, we need the doll and the pen," said Milo. "You do know that someone is going to have to die in order for her to pass the curse," said Milo.

"That's not in the plan. Quinn had me meet her at a place in the woods where Frank said that he met Ostar. That's where we are going. It could be the only way to hopefully get Ostar to show his face. Our only chance is Aubrie. I just hope that she isn't too afraid."

Milo sighed and rubbed his hand over his bald head. "Just tell me what you want me to do."

# # #

Park never missed a week of visiting his sister, Piper's grave. Even though he was absorbed in finding Ostar and stopping the curse, it did not stop him from paying his respects. Rain or shine, he was there to update Piper on what he was doing.

"Pipe, you've been gone for a couple of months now and it still hurts. It hurts more now that I know why you are gone. I'm not going to give up. I found Ostar's carrier and we are going to try to stop this curse. I just wish I knew exactly what he wants. Is he really just trying to save his world? I'm not sure but I won't stop. It is you that keeps me going. I need you to be at peace."

Park heard steps over the fallen and dried leaves coming towards him. He turned to see Samantha, his twenty-eight-year-old ex-fiancé. He was speechless and couldn't decide whether to turn his back on her as she did to him on their wedding day or to speak with her. He turned away.

"Park," she softly called, pulling her straight black hair from her face as the wind blew.

Samantha was from the Philippines and lived in Michigan since she was a child. Her parents were too young to care for her and sent her to the United States to live with her aunt and uncle who could provide a better life for her. Samantha wanted to know more about her parents but every time she thought about them, her curiosity left her feeling abandoned. When she met Park during a half marathon run, she was the happiest she could have ever been and never imagined that she would be the one to break his heart because of her fear that one day he may also abandon her.

She slipped her hands inside the pockets of her long overcoat that covered her tall thin frame. She had a look of uncertainty when Park turned away, but she understood his reluctance. She hurt him and knew he would never understand her reasoning. She couldn't understand why her fear of losing him was so strong and knew from the second she walked away leaving him crushed, that she had made a mistake.

"Park," she said again, walking close enough to gently place her hand on his shoulder.

Park pulled away and turned to face her. He had not seen or talked to her since the horrible and embarrassing day of his wedding and would have preferred to never see her again. But the moment his eyes locked onto hers, the memories of why he fell in love with her flooded back into his heart.

"Why are you here?" he questioned, feeling a lump in his throat and looking away.

"I talked to Milo," she responded.

"I know."

"I talked to Milo today. He is worried about you and so am I," she said, continuing to look at him as he kept his head turned. "He wants me, of all people, to try to talk you into seeing a doctor. And he's right, you've lost a lot of weight. Your skin is pale, Park, you need to see a doctor."

Park chuckled. "I'm fine. Look, it's nice that you guys are concerned. He should not have said anything to you. It's nothing that a little rest won't cure. And honestly Sam, you don't have the right to worry about me," he said in a bitter tone. "Not anymore."

"I'm sorry Park!" she yelled. "I'm sorry for what I did to you, I... I was scared. Nothing would have made me happier than to be your wife but then… then I would think about that knock I would get with men telling me that you were gone. The closer it got to our wedding the more it haunted me until I just couldn't do it. I couldn't breathe, I felt as if my heart was going to just stop."

Park sighed, then faced her with no emotion.

"This is what I was when we met and I didn't know how bad your abandonment issues were until you abandoned me. No matter how much I assured you, no matter how much I loved what I did, your fear of being left alone haunted you. I just wish you would have talked to someone, a professional, that could have gotten you through your fears," he said with visible pain. "You know what? I can't do this right now."

"Then when Park? Piper was like a sister to me. I hurt every day since she has been gone and I have no one to talk with about it, about her, about how she died. You won't talk to me! You couldn't even pick up your phone to let me express how sorry I was!"

"Don't make this about yourself Sam," he snapped.

"You're right," she said, lowering her voice in embarrassment. "Look, I don't want to make things worse than what it already is between us, not that it can be any worse, but please, can we talk this through? It's been almost ten months and every day I wake up knowing that I made the biggest mistake of my life. I was just so in my head about everything. I was too insecure, and I was a fool. I know that now. I wanted a family with you but my fear of raising a family alone got the best of me. I was dumb, stupid and I hate myself for what I've done not just to you, but to us."

Park's eyes filled with tears. He wiped his eyes before the tears fell down his face.

"You know me well enough to know that I don't forgive or forget easily. My heart hurts, it hasn't stopped hurting since you walked away. After I got over the anger, my heart continued to ache. It still aches, every day."

"Will you ever find it in your heart to forgive me? I am sorry."

"Don't act like we never talked about this. I never let it get in my head that I could lose you and it never scared me to the point of just walking away because of not being able to face death. You didn't give us a chance, you didn't want to."

Samantha began to sob. "I admit that it was self-sabotage on my part."

Park was guarded. "So, what do you want?"

Samantha sighed, she was relieved that he didn't walk away from her or refuse to talk.

"I want you to know that I'm here. Whatever is going on with you, I'm here. I hope you can find peace with Piper's death and as for us, I want us to talk more, something I should have asked of you a long time before we got engaged. I am seeing a therapist. She says that she thinks that this all revolves around my parents."

"Really," he said, surprised. "I think that is good. Maybe your therapist is right, about your parents. But," he said. "I can't talk about this. Not now. There is something that I must see all the way through. I'm not crazy and I can't go into it with you, but after this is all over, I'll have a clearer mind and we can have that talk."

"Okay, fair enough," she said as she turned to walk away before turning back to him with a faint smile. "I never for one second stopped loving you, Park."

Park gave a weak smile as she turned again and walked away.

CHAPTER TEN

Sydney and Aubrie called their part-time jobs at a local yogurt store a welcomed escape from being near Joan. Although Joan told them that it would teach them independence, it was really her way of filling her pockets with more money because she took half of their earnings. It wasn't fair but it was Joan's rules. Her brother owned the store which made it easy to convince him to hold their jobs until they came back from camp.

Sydney was working at the counter serving ice cream to a couple of young children while Aubrie wiped down tables and counters. Aubrie was surprised that Sydney showed up for work and on time, but she had nothing to say to her. With what she learned from the detectives, she struggled to act normal.

Two girls from their school, Skylar and Whitney, strutted into the parlor wearing tight jeans, low cut boots, white tee shirts, and varsity jackets. The two were categorized as typical popular mean girls born with silver spoons. Sydney rolled her eyes and looked at Aubrie who did the same, which was a gratifying ice breaker for the two.

"Hi Sydney, hi Aubrie," greeted blond-haired Whitney in her normal high-pitched annoying voice.

As the girls stepped to the counter, Skylar gave a disgusted look to Sydney.

"What's up with the hair?" asked Skylar, staring at Sydney's frizzy thick hair, then running her fingers through her silky dark hair. "Don't you hate the moisture in the air? Maybe you should try my hairdresser. Oh, wait! You probably couldn't afford her."

Both girls giggled while Sydney struggled to keep her temper from boiling. Aubrie dropped her rag on a table and stormed to the girls.

"You two need to order something or get out. We have to put up with your crap all day every day at school, but not here," Aubrie threatened.

Whitney turned to Aubrie and stepped close to her.

"Or what little orphan girl?" she snarled, giving Aubrie a shove.

Aubrie lost her balance and almost fell while the girls laughed.

"She's so clumsy!" exclaimed Skylar.

Sydney turned away from the girls as her pupils flashed and the whites of her eyes turned to blood. She balled her fists and began to heavily breathe.

Aubrie glanced at Sydney. She could see her breathing become deeper and deeper, and knew she had to do something. Aubrie suddenly grabbed Whitney, who was much taller, by her long hair, and wound it around her arm until she whimpered in pain and fear.

"Let me go!" Whitney cried. "Let me go, you're hurting me!"

Aubrie released Whitney and pushed her causing her

to stumble.

"You're so clumsy!" Aubrie mocked. "Get out of here!"

Whitney tried to compose herself.

"I hear your orphan mom makes you work. Wonder how she is going to react when she finds out that you both got fired! My parents will make that happen and you know it!" she cried as Skylar pulled her out of the store.

Sydney still had her back turned. Her eyes had returned to normal and her breathing was no longer erratic. Aubrie slowly approached her.

"Syd, are you okay?"

Sydney turned to Aubrie and took a deep breath.

"Yea, I'm fine. I wish those two were dead," she casually said. "They don't realize how close they came."

"Don't talk like that."

Sydney smiled, then laughed. "Well, what about you?" she joked. "I can't believe you pulled Whitney's hair!"

Aubrie began to laugh. "I know right? I figured that you would have leaped over the counter and slammed their heads against the glass, but then you turned your back on them. That's not like you to turn away from a fight."

"I was just trying to keep my cool. I'm saving my anger for when it counts and you're right, if we stay out of trouble, trouble is not going to keep following us. Though it did seem to walk right in here and find us," Sydney replied. "They think we are trash. Everyone thinks that we are trash, but I don't care."

Aubrie walked back over to the table and began wiping it down with the rag. She stopped and looked at Sydney.

"Syd. You know those marks that you drew on your hand?"

Sydney looked at the marks on her hand and said,

"Yea, what about it?"

"I think we should have a doctor take a look at it."

Sydney became suspicious. "Why would you say that? I do not need to see a doctor. It's a marker, it'll come off. What harm can my drawing on my skin with a marker do? Please, just drop it," she urged, walking around the counter to her.

"I think your behavior change has something to do with the marks on your hand," she said with caution. "Why do you keep making it darker? You've become so obsessed with it."

Sydney was aggravated. "I don't have to tell you anything! The second things get fine with us you start in again! Just leave me alone!" she screamed, walking back around the counter just as customers walked in.

She eyeballed Aubrie then put on a smile to greet the customers.

# # #

It was past midnight, both Sydney and Aubrie were sound asleep in their beds until Aubrie was awakened by Sydney's fast and loud breathing. Aubrie looked over to her and watched as the blanket covering her moved quickly up and down.

"Syd," whispered Aubrie. "Are you okay?"

Sydney did not hear her and continued breathing fast. Aubrie pulled herself from her bed and in a grog, stumbled over to see Sydney's eyes pop open filled with blood. Aubrie stood wide-eyed and frightened.

"Syd! Wake up!" she screamed, shoving her.

Sydney's eyes turned to normal as she focused on Aubrie. She didn't say a word, instead, she glared at Aubrie who was shivering in fear. She quietly crept back to her bed, knowing that Park and Milo were keeping something from her. She wrapped herself in her blanket and laid on her side facing Sydney who had turned her back to her. Sydney quickly fell asleep and began to dream.

# # #

Sydney was in the woods staring up at the bright moon through the fog when Ostar appeared wearing all black with a long coat and a hood over his long black straw-like hair.

"Sydney. Why do you hesitate?" questioned Ostar, sounding as if he were speaking underwater.

"Hesitate?"

"Yes, to send me those who forfeited their souls. You have one left, yet you do nothing," Ostar calmly said. "You must choose in order for your journey to be complete. The magic must be passed one last time before what I have been waiting for, becomes reality. Not a revival of my realm but a new realm."

Sydney chuckled. "Magic? This isn't magic. It's power. My power."

"Call it what you want Sydney," Ostar said as he neared her. "But you must finish what has been started. Send the last soul and then bring me yours. This is your destiny."

Ostar slowly strolled in a slow circle around her forcing her to continuously turn to keep sight of him. He studied her.

"You're not like the rest, not one who would even show curiosity of something so meek as a doll, yet you did. I struggle to control you, unlike your predecessors. I sense when I receive your soul, it will be more powerful than the rest. I am looking forward to it."

"It's because I am stronger willed. I understand my

destiny. I will do what you wish but in my own time."

Ostar became angry. "This is my time! Your only purpose is to finish what you've started and pass the magic!"

"Why are you doing this? Where are you from?" Sydney asked, stepping closer to him.

"No one that carries the magic has ever questioned me," said Ostar as blood seeped from his chapped lips and down his olive toned chin. "No one questions me!"

"I do," she said with no fear.

"As I said, you're vastly different than any of my carriers. Why would that be?" he asked, slowly shifting his head from side to side with a curious expression. "What makes you so defiant even under my spell?"

Sydney glared at the demon who for the first time had an indecisive look, unable to understand how she had so much control. He knew that until she sent him her soul, he was almost powerless and that angered him.

"You've had many... opportunities... to find a soul to send to me. Many have angered you Sydney. We are too close to the end for this to have been for nothing. Send me a soul!"

"Why do you take our souls?"

"I don't take them, they are given to me."

"Right, forfeited."

Ostar appeared confused. "You cannot see the purpose? Everyone sees the purpose. You baffle me."

"I see nothing but the trees and the ground, and you."

Ostar spread his arms wide and looked down to the ground.

"This is our destiny, Sydney. I share this with you. What lies beneath, is our old world."

Ostar's eyes began to bleed as he looked into Sydney's eyes. She then looked down to see deep beneath the earth, mounds of skeletons.

"Once you pass the magic, there will be only 4 souls left and the bones you see will come to life. My kingdom and our new world will live again."

Ostar smiled, cracking his lips even further.

"You will be a part of the power from a resurrected world, through me. But you need to finish your journey."

"In time Ostar," Sydney said with a sneaky smirk, turning away from him. "I'm not quite ready."

CHAPTER ELEVEN

"Thanks for coming," Park said as Aubrie hopped in his car and shut the door.

He was waiting for her outside a convenience store near where the girls lived, hoping that she had gotten his text message to meet him.

"We are running out of time. Did you find the doll? When can you get it to me?"

Aubrie sighed. "I know where it is," she said with fear in her voice. "I'm scared."

Park remained calm but stern. "I get it, but there's no one else we can turn to. You must help us. I'm trying to not only stop the transfer of this curse to the last carrier but..."

Park's eyes widened and he suddenly stopped speaking. He turned his head to the side window and bit his bottom lip, angry with himself.

"Curse? What? Why did you say that?"

Park rubbed his temples and said, "Nothing, I'm just feeling like this is a curse. It came out wrong."

"But you said transfer of this curse to the last carrier. That's not something that just comes out wrong," she suspiciously commented. "Transfer to who? What carrier?"

There was awkward silence as Park looked around the area outside of the store trying to figure out what to say.

"This isn't some sort of man-made chemical is it?" she questioned. "Or rather not the kind that you want me to believe. You do think it's a curse, don't you? I know it's a curse based on what I saw last night."

"What did you see?" Park asked, lowering his head and fighting the pain that was becoming more frequent in his head.

"Are you okay?" Aubrie asked.

"I'm fine, what did you see?"

"Her eyes," she said softly. "They bled."

"What?"

"She was asleep, or at least I think she was asleep. Her eyes were open and it looked like she blew out the vessels in her eyes. Then it disappeared," she said. "What is happening?"

Park leaned back in his seat and looked at the ceiling of his car. He lost his thought for a moment when his eyes froze on the smear of makeup that Samantha wore. She frequently drove his car and when she pulled the visor down, it seemed to always be right after she touched her face, leaving a stain. He cleaned it regularly but hadn't done so since she left him.

"We think the pen carries the blood of a demon... Ostar, he's evil," he said, finally pulling his attention from the sight of the smudge on the ceiling. "We're not sure exactly what he wants but when that ink gets on the skin, that person becomes..." Park sighed when Aubrie interrupted him.

"Possessed?" Aubrie figured, taking a deep breath.

"And more," Park replied.

"Tell me what it is. It's like she is under a spell, she won't eat, and her temper goes from warm to hot in a second. No one notices it because that's just who she is. We spend all our time together, since we were young, and I can see that she is a lot worse than she's ever been. Why is this happening to her?"

"It's our souls. He wants them, but they must come to him by his blood, through people like Sydney. They find three people and influence them to take their own lives and when they are dead, their souls go to Ostar," Park explained. "When they get mad and I mean really mad at someone, they attack by cutting their face. It somehow transfers Ostar's blood into them and controls them to commit suicide and people think it's exactly that, suicide. I don't know how to save Sydney, but we can't do anything without that pen, and it is up to you to get it. I hate to have you do this, but you're the only one that can."

"How do you know so much about this?" she asked.

Park cleared his throat and blurted, "My sister, she was one of Ostar's victims and I've seen first-hand what this curse can do, what the carrier can do."

Aubrie was stunned as she listened to Park.

"So, it wasn't my imagination," she said. "What I saw last night, Sydney's eyes. It happened."

"It was real."

"Why their souls?"

"It's what he needs to bring life back to his world, at least that is what I was told. We can't be a hundred percent sure on any of this," Park replied. "Aubrie, please, this is the only way we can try to stop this. Sydney was responsible for a woman's death that happened the night that you told us that she left the camp."

"Oh my God!" she said in a panic.

"I'm sure you've heard of Holden Griggs."

"The big drug dealer? Yes, we saw on the news that he was killed."

"He was Sydney's father,"

Aubrie dropped her jaw. "That's why she was so upset."

"She was also responsible for the death of the detective that killed him," he added.

"The guy that lit himself on fire?" she questioned in shock. "It was all over social media. This is insane!"

"She's going to attack one more time and pass the doll with the pen, to someone else. We've gotta get to it before that happens," he explained. "Once she passes the doll... she's going to kill herself. We need to do this tonight."

Aubrie was terrified. She took a deep breath.

"Okay, I'll get it. Then what?"

"You call me right away and meet me right here," he instructed. "But before you leave the house open the back of the doll and make sure the pen is there but do not touch it, no matter what. She will know."

"Okay," Aubrie said, looking through the side window. "I need to get back home before anyone notices that I am gone."

"You can do this. Just call me the second you are out of the house and I'll be here waiting," he said to her as she got out of the car.

"Okay," she said, jogging away.

Park squinted his eyes and rubbed his temples to ease the stabbing pain in his head. He knew he needed to hold on until he could beat Ostar. He reached into his inside jacket pocket and pulled out a prescription bottle. He took a pill out and popped it in his mouth before leaving.

# # #

"How did it go with Aubrie?" Milo asked, sitting beside Park at the bar of a restaurant near the convenience store where he met Aubrie.

Milo observed Park's attire and smiled at his cleaned-up friend.

The bartender approached, placing a basket of fries, condiments, and two small plates in front of them.

"Thank you," said Park to the bartender before turning to Milo. "I got enough for you."

Milo grabbed a plate and dished out fries.

"Not a healthy meal but glad to see you eating something," he said.

"I finally have a bit of an appetite," Park replied, taking fries from the basket and shoving them in his mouth.

"They do serve burgers and sandwiches," Milo suggested.

Park gave a grim smile. "The fries will do, and it went ok with Aubrie, she's terrified but she will have the doll tonight. I'm just waiting for her to call."

"I sure hope that you have some sort of a plan because I don't."

"I do," said Park with a grin. "But you're probably not going to like it."

Milo stopped chewing and stared at Park who had a serious look on his face.

"I'm pretty sure no matter what the plan, I'm not going to like it," he said. "Spit it out."

"Once I have the doll from Aubrie, I need you to meet

me in the woods outside of Jackson Park. My car will be about a half mile past the entrance sign."

"That's on the border of Frasier and Cliff County, why out there?"

"It's the same place where Frank saw Ostar and it's far enough away from the public."

"Don't you think that's dangerous? We have no idea what he will do, if he shows up, not to mention what we will do," Milo complained.

"You don't have to come, Milo," Park said.

"Oh yes I do," he replied.

Park sighed. "This is the only way to bring him out, or rather, I hope. We'll have the doll and he's going to want what's inside," Park explained.

"If Sydney hasn't found the last soul to send to him, there's no telling what he's going to do," Milo commended with concern, rubbing the chills from his arms.

"She holds the power. She's gotta send him that soul. Until then, it doesn't seem that he can do anything, otherwise he would have done something weeks ago to force her to do it."

"And what about Sydney? What if this goes south and she winds up finding us in the woods?"

Park sighed. "That's where you will come in," he said. "I think we need to drive separately, just in case."

"In case something goes wrong," Milo confirmed. "Agreed."

# # #

Aubrie arrived home before anyone noticed that she was gone. She trotted up to her room to see Sydney sitting on her bed. Aubrie found it difficult to act as if everything was fine and avoided talking as much as she could. When Sydney was home, she was always in their bedroom and most of the time she would sit as if she were hypnotized staring at the walls. As she was about to close the door, she heard Joan call from downstairs.

"Everyone! Time for dinner. We are all eating at the dinner table together," she called. "If you're not down in 5 minutes, you won't eat."

"The warden calls. She must have worn out the bell and lost her mind. Now we are forced to sit with her at the dinner table," Aubrie said in humor.

Sydney snapped from her daze, stood, and looked at her, giving a chuckle. Aubrie was pleasantly surprised.

"You go," said Sydney. "I'm not hungry and I hope for your sake that she didn't burn whatever she's serving this time."

"Hungry or not Syd, you have to go down. If she thinks something is wrong with you, she's going to immediately think you're on drugs and then you're stuck in a medical clinic peeing in a cup and waiting to get blood work. Honestly, that's not a bad idea. We can find out what's going on with you and if nothing is wrong, I can stop harping on you about those marks on your hand."

"I definitely won't be seeing a doctor, so, let's go," Sydney said, opening the door wider.

Aubrie laughed. "I'll be down in a couple of minutes, I need to change first. Save me a seat."

"Sure," Sydney responded as she left the room and headed down the stairs.

It was now or never, Aubrie thought, before frantically opening Sydney's bag to see the doll. Her hands were shaking as she lifted it. She turned it over and opened the back, revealing the pen. She closed it and put the doll in her backpack before quickly sending a text to Park.

Quietly, she lifted her bedroom window and climbed out, scaling her way down to the ground. She and Sydney were experts at sneaking out of the house from their bedroom and the experience paid off, she was on the ground in no time. She ran as fast as she could to the convenience store parking lot and waited a few minutes before seeing Park's car. She hopped in clinging to her backpack.

"Wait, what are you doing Aubrie?" Park asked confused. "Just give me the doll."

"I'm going with you," Aubrie blurted, sliding her bag to her side and away from Park.

"I can't have you part of this, it's too dangerous, now give it to me," Park ordered, getting angry.

"I can either open this doll and touch the pen or you can start driving. I'm going with you. I can't let Sydney get hurt and I need to know that this thing exists, for real."

"Aubrie, please, this is not a game. This is real and it's too dangerous. Milo and I will make sure Sydney doesn't get hurt. If this goes as planned, the only one we'll see and destroy is Ostar."

Aubrie reared back in her seat looking ahead with a straight face. Park realized that she was not going to get out of the car and he couldn't risk her threat.

"May as well relax, this is quite the drive," Park said, looking at her and then at the backpack that she continued to keep away from his reach.

Aubrie was nervous and could feel her heart pounding. She closed her eyes and remained silent as they drove away.

While Park and Aubrie headed to the woods, Sydney sat at the dinner table with the other kids wondering why Aubrie hadn't come down. Joan stepped in carrying a bowl of dinner rolls and sat it on the table.

"I know this isn't normal for all of us to eat together, but I felt that it was time for a change and maybe we could all share what's going on in our lives," she said with a smile, something she rarely did. "Where's Aubrie?"

She looked around at everyone at the table who were hunching their shoulders and looking at each other.

"I thought she was coming down. She said she needed to change," Sydney announced, standing. "I'll go see where she is."

"Sit down Sydney. She knows the rules, she heard my call," scolded Joan.

"I'm not hungry, I'm going back to my room," she said with sass as she walked away.

"Don't come back later to eat, you know the rules too," lectured Joan.

Sydney ignored her and ran up the stairs and into an empty bedroom. Aubrie was gone. She looked down noticing that her duffel bag was open and rummaged through. She pulled it further open and began searching for the doll, but it wasn't there. She knew Aubrie took it but was not sure why, nor where she was going with it. She clenched her fists in fury as her pupils flashed and her eyes filled with blood. Until Aubrie touched the pen, she would not know where she was. All she could do was wait.

It had been half an hour and no word of where Aubrie was. Joan stomped into the bedroom where Sydney was pacing.

"Where is Aubrie? You two need to clean up the kitchen."

Sydney stepped close to Joan showing no fear.

"We never make the mess, but you make us clean it up. Your real kids are the slobs and you think we are the hired help and your kids act as if we are beneath them. Make them clean it up!"

Joan crimped her lips.

"I don't have to justify or explain anything to you or Aubrie, but when you do bad things and make life miserable for those around you, you pay the consequences with hopes that you have learned a lesson. You and Aubrie will either get your act together and prove to me that you're heading on the right track or you'll keep doing as you're doing and continue to clean up after everyone else regardless if you made the mess or not!" she yelled. "Now, where is Aubrie?"

"I... don't... know," Sydney said in a slow and eerie tone. "Why don't you do what you always do and track her phone?"

Joan glared at her and then stormed out.

CHAPTER TWELVE

Aubrie remained silent for the entire drive until they arrived at the outskirts of the woods.

"Would you at least stay in the car?" Park asked as he turned the engine off.

Aubrie stepped out of the car with the backpack over her shoulder, ignoring him. The moon illuminated the trees making it less eerie and while not regretting her decision to accompany Park, she still had an uneasy feeling. She was frightened and even startled as Park came from behind her with his hand held out.

"The doll," said Park.

Aubrie took control of her fear with a deep breath before opening her backpack and handing the doll to him.

"Now what?" Aubrie quietly asked, looking around.

"We wait," he said, walking further into the woods.

"For how long?"

"As long as it takes," he replied, reaching in his

pocket, pulling out the key fob to his car, and handing it to Aubrie.

"If this goes bad, you need to promise me that you'll get in my car and leave."

"I promise. But what are you going to do?"

Park ignored her question and stopped walking.

"Right here is where it all started. It's where Ostar showed himself and I plan on staying here, with this doll until he shows his face."

"And then what?"

Park gave a nervous chuckle as he pulled out a collection bag with blood in it.

"Is that blood?" she asked as her eyes widened.

"Yes, it's mine. We don't know if it will work but we have to try. If Ostar appears, this will be waiting for him."

"If he knows you're here with the pen, won't Sydney?"

"She will if we touch it and if that happens, she'll be here twenty times faster than it took us. Milo will be here shortly," he said. "I know that I can't talk you into taking my car and going home, so stay close to me and if I tell you to run, you run. I just don't know how this is going to turn out."

Aubrie nodded.

"I want to stay. It's all so unbelievable and at the same time remarkable. I have to stay. And what if Milo doesn't make it? You won't have a car to get home."

"He'll be here," Park quickly responded.

"I'm not leaving," Aubrie said, looking into Park's eyes.

"Come on then, we'll wait for Milo by my car.

Park and Aubrie slowly walked back to the street outside the woods waiting for Milo and not saying a word to each other for almost twenty minutes. They suddenly saw a small car speeding to them and screeching to a halt behind Park's car.

"Aubrie!" yelled Joan as she exited the car and stormed in a rage towards her.

Both Aubrie and Park were shocked to see her. Park discreetly slid the bag with his blood from his pocket and dropped it in the seat of the car.

"You're following me?" Aubrie questioned in disgust.

"Why are you out here Aubrie? It took a long time for me to get out here and even longer once I lost reception. I have been driving all over to find you! If you want me to ever stop tracking you on your phone then stop running off without permission!"

"Why do you even care? You must be afraid that you're going to lose part of your income if you lose me, right?"

"You are pressing your luck. Now get in the car!" she yelled as she furiously approached Park. "What the hell are you doing out here with her! She's sixteen! I knew something was off about you. I'll be reporting you!"

"Ma'am, I needed Aubrie's help to get..."

Joan looked down to see the doll in Park's hand and snatched it from him.

"What is this?"

"Give that back!" Park exclaimed, trying to get it from her.

He firmly grabbed her arm and tried to grab the doll, but Joan struggled with him until the back of the doll came open. She saw the strange looking pen and immediately touched it.

"Aubrie! Get out of here! Now!" Park yelled to Aubrie who was frozen with fear. "Aubrie go! There isn't much time!"

Park turned to Joan and reached for the doll. "Give me the doll, please Joan."

Joan jerked away still holding it and before another word could be said or anyone could take another step, Sydney rushed to them. She was outraged. Her pupils flashed and the whites of her eyes filled with blood.

"Give it to me!" she bellowed with a deepened voice.

"Sydney stop!" cried Aubrie. "Don't do this!"

"Do what?" snarled Joan with a firm grip on the doll. "Someone tell me what the hell is going on!"

Sydney snapped her attention to Aubrie and shouted, "It's my destiny!"

Park tried to remain calm. "Sydney, I know you killed Sara Malor and the detective that took your father's life. Who's next? One of us, right? Ostar is tired of waiting."

"Yes, I helped that bitch and that cop forfeit their souls. They deserved it," Sydney admitted with a cocky smile. "We were going to be a family and she ruined everything!"

# # #

Sara was startled when she heard someone banging on her front door. The pounding was so loud that she hesitated to answer it, but when she looked through the peephole, she saw a young, frightened girl.

"Are you alright?" she asked, opening the door widely. "It's quite late for you to be out."

"I was trying to get home, but my car died, I can't reach my dad because my phone died too. It's so dark out that I got scared. I saw your light on and thought I would see if you would let me use your phone or if you would call my dad for me."

"You poor thing," said Sara in a sympathetic tone. "Come in, it's chilly out and you're not dressed appropriately for this weather."

She guided the girl into the entrance of the house and picked up her phone that sat on a table near the door.

"Okay, who is your father, and what's his number? I will call

him and assure him that you are safe. You can stay here until he arrives."

Sydney was silent for a moment but could feel her blood begin to boil in anger.

"What's your name? It's okay," she said with comfort.

"My name is Sydney. My father's name is... Holden... Griggs."

Sara glared at Sydney and slowly lowered the phone.

"What? Holden has no daughter. Who are you?"

"Oh yes he does, he wrote to me and told me all about you. He wrote about how wonderful you were, how he was going to marry you, and how he wanted to tell you about me with hopes that you'd be happy to have me," she said, speaking quickly. "We were supposed to be a family and I was going to have my dad!"

"I want you out of my house," she snarled. "Now!"

Sara opened the door, but Sydney slammed it in a rage as her pupils flashed and her eyes filled with blood.

Sara was mortified. She dropped her phone on the floor and covered her mouth with her hands.

"You ruined it all, Sara! He told me that you confronted him about his business!" she cried in fury. "You shouldn't have broken his heart and I'm not going to let you get away with it!"

Sydney lunged at her, slit her face with her nail, and pushed her away causing her to stumble in a daze.

Sara immediately turned and walked through the hallway to the kitchen, taking her car key fob from a rack. She then walked out of the door that led to the garage with Sydney following. She wiped the blood that seeped from her wound before it could drop to the floor and then calmly pulled a garden hose that was neatly wound on the floor and a roll of duct tape from a shelf. As if she were working on a home project, she knelt in front of the exhaust pipe of the car and carefully placed the hose inside and wrapped it tightly with the tape.

Sydney peered at the woman who took the other end of the hose and opened the driver's side of the car. She got in, started it, and rolled the window down enough for the hose to be inserted inside. She then got out and took her time placing the duct tape around the hose and over the opening of the window, making sure that it was completely sealed. Still in a trance, she walked to the passenger side of the car and got in. She shut the door and closed her eyes as the exhaust filled the inside of the car.

Sydney stood at the door that led to the garage and waited until she was sure that she was dead. She peeked in for one last look as her eyes returned to normal. She then calmly walked back into the house and out the front door.

# # #

"That cop deserved what he got too, he killed my father!"

"Your father was going to kill another man, in cold blood! He couldn't let that happen!" Park shouted. "Your father took a lot of lives, and so has Ostar!"

"That's not true! Everyone was out to get my father!" she screamed. "This power, this strength… it truly was a gift, and without it, they would have never gotten what they deserved."

"What's Ostar's plan, Sydney?" Park asked, making sure to keep his distance from her. "Tell me how to stop him."

Sydney looked down at the ground and gave a look of joy. Aubrie and Joan kept their distance from Sydney but both were paralyzed by what was happening.

"Why would I do that? It is all right here, under our feet. We are bringing them back to life and our world will be his."

Park was confused. "What?"

Joan had enough of what she was hearing and became angry.

"What the hell is going on Sydney!" scolded Joan who stood in front of Aubrie. "What are we all doing out here?"

Sydney leaped at Joan, snatched her away from Aubrie, and quickly slit her cheek. Aubrie watched in shock as Sydney threw Joan to the ground causing the doll to fly from her hands and land at Park's feet. He quickly picked it up.

Joan scuffled to stand. She looked around for a moment to compose herself, then focused on one of the many trees that stood deeper into the woods and ran to it. She gazed up at the tree before wrapping her arms and legs around the trunk.

"Joan!" Aubrie called. "What are you doing!"

Park ran to the tree to try to stop her from climbing. Aubrie followed behind leaving Sydney watching with excitement.

Park grabbed Joan's ankle but a fierce kick to his face forced him to release her. They could only watch as she silently made her way up the tree. She was calm as she quickly navigated to the other side, away from everyone. She spread her arms wide and let herself fall before anyone could shift to catch her. Park ran to her discovering that her neck was broken. She was gone. He shielded Aubrie from the gruesome sight before turning his attention back to Sydney who approached them. She was breathing heavily with a look of desperation.

"I need the doll. It must be passed. It is the last time. I'm passing it for the last time. Ostar's realm will live," she said with a pause. "Here."

Park's eyes widened in shock. "Here? That's his end game? He wants our world?"

Sydney smiled. Her eyes were still filled with blood and her pupils continued to flash.

"It just needs to be passed one more time and when the journey is complete, Ostar will be king again and in time this world will be his new world and we will all be a part of it. We will resurrect and carry the magic that will forfeit all human souls. We've come too far to have it stop now. I don't want to hurt you, but I will. I've almost completed my part. The doll that carries the blood of Ostar must be passed," she said as her voice became deeper and fierce. "You can't stop this!"

Sydney lunged at Park, knocking him over causing him to drop the doll. She picked it up and stepped away from him as he scampered to get distance from her before he stood.

"Sydney!" screamed Aubrie. "Please! Do not do this! We're a team, remember?"

Sydney's eyes returned to normal. She gave Aubrie a sorrowful look before she raised her arm. As she was about to hurl the doll, Milo sprinted to her and knocked her over before she could throw it. Sydney fell to the ground with her head landing on a large stone. She was lifeless as blood trickled from the back of her head.

Park ran to Sydney and grabbed the doll that had fallen from her hand and then rushed to Aubrie.

"Aubrie, take my car and as soon as you get reception, call for help."

Aubrie was in shock. Park took hold of her shoulders and shook her.

"Aubrie, I need you to go and get help," he said in a calm tone. "Go."

Milo knelt in front of Sydney and placed his fingers on her neck. His eyes widened as he looked back to Park.

"She's still alive Park! Her pulse is weak but it's there!" he exclaimed.

Park looked at Milo then back to Aubrie and with a stern voice, he said, "Aubrie, go. When you get about five miles out, you should have reception by then and you can call for help. Can you do that?"

Aubrie shivered in fear as Park gave her a gentle nudge. She nodded, then ran to Park's car, got in, and sped away.

Park watched until he could no longer see the rear lights of the car. He turned and slowly walked to Milo who was sitting beside Sydney.

"I can't believe this," said Milo in shock. "What do we say? How do we explain what happened to that woman over there? She threw herself from that tree, I saw this girl's eyes, I saw it all. How the hell are we going to explain this and what are we going to do with that doll and most importantly, the pen?"

Park put his hands on his hips. "I don't know. But we gotta get our story straight about all of this before this place gets flooded with police."

"What about her?"

"We can't move her, but help will be here soon," Park replied.

"She has to take her life to continue the curse," said Milo. "I hate to even think it, but our best bet is if she never wakes up, ever."

Park's eyes widened.

"What are you saying? Kill her?" he blurted, looking at Sydney and then at the doll. "We can't kill her, we only want to kill Ostar. Maybe she won't wake up. If she never wakes up, she can't take her life. We need to see how this all turns out with her. But we are not murderers."

"It's the only way Park. You know it!"

"I don't care what she's become. We're not going to take her life!" Park shouted in disgust.

Milo stood, faced Park, and said, "If she survives and succeeds, we've lost. You heard what Tom said. He had the doll and this thing found it. We have a chance right now to end this!"

"No!" Park shouted. "She didn't ask for this, she's still a human being."

Milo sighed and turned back to the girl.

"Then we have to pray that she doesn't make it. She can't wake up."

While Milo hoped that Sydney would not survive, his compassion forced him to place his jacket against the wound on her head and apply pressure to stop the bleeding. Park became fixated on the blood and fell into deep concentration. Milo noticed.

"What?" he questioned.

Park looked through the trees and could faintly see his car. He realized he was too far away to retrieve what he needed which was the blood. He looked down at his palm.

"Do you still carry that pocketknife?" he asked as he knelt.

Milo gave a grin and said, "The only time it's not on me is when I'm in the shower."

He pulled the knife from the pocket of his jeans and handed it to Park. Park immediately opened it and slid the blade across his palm, cuffing his hand as his blood seeped from the wound. He gently removed Milo's jacket from Sydney's head and let the blood from his hand drop into the gash at the back of her skull.

"Quinn did this to reverse the curse on her babysitter and it worked," Park explained.

Milo's face brightened. "This could be it?"

"I know that it works on the victims, but I don't know if it will work on the carrier. It's a long shot but at least we'll know," he said, putting the jacket back over her head. "Keep applying pressure."

Park looked to the sky and began turning in circles.

Blood from his hand ran down his fingers and to the ground.

"Ostar! I have the doll and more importantly, the pen! She still has her soul and you're not going to get it!" he screamed, holding the doll to the sky. "I have your blood inside this doll! You lose Ostar! You hear me! You lose! Show yourself! I'm right here!"

Park waited and waited, looking up through the trees. There was no sign of Ostar.

CHAPTER THIRTEEN

Less than an hour later, a helicopter safely landed in an open space outside of the woods. Police cars and ambulances were stopped near Milo and Joan's cars.

Sydney was quickly stabilized and secured on a backboard. Four men walked briskly with her to one of the ambulances that raced her to the awaiting helicopter.

Milo and Park walked back into the woods where Joan's body was being studied by a medical examiner. Their captain, a tall and lanky man, was standing over the body when he noticed Milo and Park. He approached them. Park kept the doll hidden inside his jacket.

"Park, under any other circumstances, I would say that it's good to see you. What was going on out here and how does it involve you? You're supposed to be on leave. And Milo, I am very curious to know why you are here with him. In the woods of all places. Who is that woman? How did this happen to her?"

Park struggled to find words. The captain looked at Milo.

"How did that woman wind up dead and how did the girl that's being life-flighted to the hospital end up with a busted head?" he asked with a raised voice.

"To help me and my friend Sydney get away from our foster mom, Joan," a voice suddenly said. It was Aubrie.

"And you are?" asked the captain.

"My name is Aubrie Johnson and my friend, Sydney, is in the helicopter. I am the one that called for help and they were just trying to help us get away from her," she said, pointing to Joan's body. "She was our foster mom and she brought us out here to supposedly teach us a lesson. She was going to make us find our way back home."

"How do you know these two detectives? How were you able to seek their help?"

Aubrie began to look around, searching for words.

"I found her outside the precinct a couple of days ago, she looked scared," explained Milo. "I asked her what was wrong and she told me about Joan. I... I suggested that she come inside the station with me and she said she had to get back home before she got in trouble. So, I gave her my card and told her to call me if she ever needed help, and she did. Park was with me when I got her call."

Park sighed and continued, "We tracked her phone but lost the signal a few miles before we made it here. We just kept driving until we saw Joan's car."

"When we got here," Park added. "Joan and Sydney were both up in the tree."

"Sydney climbed the tree to get away from her and Joan went after her, she was so mad," said Aubrie. "And they both fell."

The captain gave a confused look and turned to Milo.

"Milo, Park, I need you two and this young lady at the station in two hours. I know it's late, but we need to get to the bottom of this while everything is fresh in your heads," he said, walking back to the dead woman's body.

# # #

Park, Milo, and Aubrie sat in the waiting room of the hospital hoping for good news with Sydney. Aubrie could only think about what her life would be like without her, while Park worried about what was to come. Had Sydney died the moment her head struck the rock, the cycle would have been broken and Ostar and his realm would be no more, Park thought. Sydney was hanging on and all they could do was wait for updates on her condition.

The kids from the foster home along with Joan's biological children were immediately removed from the house. Joan's children were sent to live with other family members while the foster children, including Aubrie, were sent to new homes.

"No one is going to ever believe what we just saw," said Aubrie who had buried her head in her arms on her lap. "Syd has got to make it through this."

Aubrie sat between the two detectives. Milo glanced at Park and gestured for him to step away with him.

"Aubrie, we'll be right back. Do you want anything? Pop, chips?"

Aubrie didn't respond. She kept her head buried in her arms. Milo and Park walked to the corner of the corridor.

"Have you given any thought to what will happen if she pulls through?" Milo asked.

"She's going to need the doll and she'll never find it."

"Where's the pen?"

"I still have it on me, in the doll," Park answered, patting the pocket of his jacket. "I feel bad for Aubrie. I told the childcare services counselor that I would drop her off at her new foster home later."

"It's horrible just thinking, let alone saying, that our best-case scenario is for Sydney not to make it," said Milo.

Park sighed. "There is a chance that my blood reversed the curse on her," he said, glancing at Aubrie.

Aubrie was exhausted but refused to leave until she could see Sydney. At that moment, a doctor walked into the waiting room.

"For Sydney Gaines," called the doctor.

Aubrie abruptly stood. Milo and Park approached.

"Yes," said Park.

"She is on life support," said the doctor sadly.

"Oh no!" Aubrie cried.

"The court will decide when to take her off."

"And that's it!" Aubrie said in hysterics. "She's dead? She's never going to wake up? I need to see her!"

"Of course, I'll take you now. Gentlemen, you can wait here."

The doctor escorted Aubrie to Sydney's room while Milo and Park sat in the waiting room unsure what to think of the doctor's news.

"You heard what he said. She may never wake up," Milo whispered.

"As long as she stays in a coma, she will never be able to take her life, Ostar can't do anything, whatever he was planning is over. Done," said Park somberly.

"What about Aubrie? How do you think she is going to do, knowing what she knows?"

"I don't know. She seems to be a strong kid, but that is her only friend laying in that room. She's going to need a lot of time. Hopefully her new foster parents are normal and will be able to give her what she needs, and I'll check in on her. In a couple of years, she'll be an adult and free to do or go wherever she wants. I think she has a chance."

"It's good that you are going to keep in touch with her, she needs someone that she can trust," Milo said, patting him on his shoulder. "She will need someone who saw what she saw. Let her know that I'm here too."

"She saved our asses with the captain tonight. Though her convincing lie is a bit scary," Park said with a chuckle.

"Thank God the captain took pity on Aubrie and didn't keep us long in his office. And it wasn't a complete lie, just a bit stretched when it came to Joan. She did seem like the perfect mix between Mommy Dearest and Misery."

"All that matters is that he believed it," said Park.

"This sucks for Sydney. She has no one to make the decision except the courts of when to take her off life support."

"None of these people deserved what Ostar did to them," Park added.

Milo placed a hand on Park's shoulder. "I've gotta get some sleep, you should too. And tomorrow, you get yourself in to see a doctor."

"You got it. I'll let Aubrie spend a little more time with Sydney before I take her home."

Milo walked away and Park strolled through the corridor looking for Sydney's room. He could hear Aubrie's voice as he neared and found her sitting beside Sydney's bed holding her hand and crying. He stood to the side of the door so that she would not know he was there, but he listened.

"I can't believe any of this. If only that lady hadn't given you that stupid doll, you would not be here with all these tubes sticking out of you. I am so sorry. Nobody knows you like I do and all the cops, judges, and foster parents that we've seen will never know how sweet, kind, and generous you really are. We both just got dealt a couple of bad cards. Maybe you're the lucky one. You're not going to ever have to worry about where you'll end up," she sniffled. "They're probably going to take you off these machines soon and then you can rest. Could even be tomorrow and I think that Park is torn between hoping for you to survive and knowing that if you die, the chain of this curse is broken. He worries that if you do wake up from this, that you will kill yourself and your soul will go to Ostar. But he has the doll that holds that pen and he is never going to let it out of his sight. I promise you, it's safe. Forever."

Aubrie stood and leaned to Sydney's head and kissed her cheek. Park quickly walked away from the room.

CHAPTER FOURTEEN

"I am glad that you came back in to see me, Park," said Dr. Scone, an older short chubby man with thick grey hair.

He stepped outside of his office with Park and into the corridor. "I have given you all the information that you need again, and it is up to you to decide how you want to proceed. I know it was a lot to swallow when we first discussed this. This isn't going away but, it's not too late."

Park had a look of despair as he glanced over the doctor's shoulder to the nameplate on his office door that read 'Dr. Ryan Scone, Oncology'. This was really happening, he thought.

"You just can't take too much longer to make that decision. I'll need to come up with a plan for you should you choose surgery and treatment."

Park's brain was in a fog, all of what the doctor explained to him was too much. He knew something was wrong before he first saw the doctor and he did not want it to be real. He needed time to absorb what was wrong and what he was about to face. He also didn't want anything to interfere with his quest to stop Ostar, no matter the cost.

"I know this is a big blow and hard to hear, especially after losing your sister. I can give you the number of someone that you can talk to. Someone that can help you make the right decision and get you through this," suggested the doctor.

Park continued to stare at the door. He was paralyzed as thoughts of his parents, his dead sister, and even Samantha ran through his head. Cancer, no one wants to hear those words, yet it is exactly what he heard. How could he tell his parents that another one of their children could be buried before them? When would he be lying next to his sister in a cold grave, he wondered, and who would visit them? He did not know if he could ever tell the woman that shattered his heart that yes, she probably would have been a widow. How ironic he thought.

"Park," Dr. Scone said loudly as he placed a hand on his shoulder. "We can still beat this."

Park looked at him and took a deep breath.

"Yeah," he said discouraged. "Thank you, Doctor. Let's do the surgery and start treatment. Thanks for the prescription."

Park reached his car and drove straight to a pharmacy where he went in and waited for his prescription of pain medication to be filled. He beat Ostar and he needed to use the same determination to stop the pain that he had in his head.

# # #

Park had been through turmoil since the day he met

Frank and was forced to believe the unthinkable. He was getting weaker and since his mind was not occupied by the curse, he was able to see that his body was slowly deteriorating. His head hurt constantly, and medication could only take the edge off. But finally, he was ready for a new battle, a fight for his life, and what better way to kick off his new journey than hosting an epic party.

No one other than Park and Milo knew the true reason for the party but telling their friends that they saved the world by stopping a curse would have landed them next to Tom in the psychiatric hospital. Park was happy that everyone showed up after announcing that the party was the last hurrah before he would have surgery on his brain to beat the cancer.

Every room in Park's house was lit up. Cars were parked on both sides of the street and around the house, and many were still showing up.

Park was in the kitchen with a few other people talking and laughing. He had not felt that good in a long time nor drank as much as he had that night. Although his sister was gone, he stopped Ostar from bringing pain to other families. Whatever plan Ostar truly had, it was no more.

Milo approached Park carrying a bottle of beer.

"Great party, I didn't know you had this many friends or did you hire them all?" Milo asked in humor.

"This is my way of thanking every one of them, especially you, for putting up with my craziness for weeks and weeks," Park said. "So, now that you know that demons do exist, what's life going to be like for you going forward."

Milo gulped his beer, then took a deep breath and exhaled.

"I still can't fully wrap my head around it all, but for me, it was like some weird therapy to help me realize that

I'm not a freak and I'm not crazy. I'm going to take this day to day. Have you heard from Aubrie? Anything new with Sydney?"

"I talked to her earlier today. This has got to be hard for her, she is so loyal to her friend. Every moment she can, she is at her bedside. It's been three days. Her foster parents seem pretty cool. They know this will not go on for much longer, so they have been dropping her off at the hospital after school and letting her stay until visiting hours are over. I did hear that they will be taking her off life support any time now."

Milo was relieved. "This could be over soon, and Aubrie is safe."

"I hope she will be okay. I know she and Sydney were best friends and Aubrie looked up to her, but I think she will do better on her own. Sydney was a big influence on her. She carried a lot of resentment and she couldn't let it go. Aubrie seems to want to put her awful past behind her."

"And the pen?"

"It's safe," said Park, as he looked over Milo's shoulder to see Samantha entering.

Milo turned to see her and looked back at Park with a surprised look and defensively said, "I had nothing to do with it."

"I invited her," Park said with a chuckle, slapping his back and walking away to greet her.

Park slowly approached Samantha who stood in a corner watching him.

"I was hoping you would stop by," he said, leaning against the wall beside her.

"Thank you for inviting me," she said. "At least I know you kept my number."

Park smiled. "Look," he said, "I don't want to have

that conversation tonight but..."

"It's okay Park, I'm not here for that. I just wanted to see you and I want you to know that I am here for you. Whatever you need to help you get through this. Tonight is just to have a good time, okay?"

"Can I get you a drink?

"I know my way around. I see a lot of people that I haven't seen since..." she said, embarrassed. "I'll go say hi."

# # #

It was nearly two o'clock in the morning. Sydney was not going to recover and with the decision to take her off life support, Aubrie was allowed to stay with her until the end. She had fallen asleep in a chair beside Sydney's hospital bed holding her hand when suddenly Sydney grasped Aubrie's hand, startling her.

"Syd," Aubrie whispered.

Although Aubrie wanted nothing more than to have her friend back, she feared how she would be if she woke. She stood and leaned to her face.

"Syd," she said again.

Sydney's eyes suddenly opened wide as if something scared her. Aubrie's face brightened for a brief moment until her eyes closed again, releasing her grip on Aubrie's hand.

Aubrie reached over Sydney and pressed a button to call for the nurse who immediately came in.

"She squeezed my hand and her eyes opened!" Aubrie exclaimed, breathing fast with excitement.

"I don't think so. You look so tired, you probably imagined it," said the nurse in a comforting tone.

"She opened her eyes! I saw it!" Aubrie yelled.

"Calm down Aubrie, calm down," said the nurse as

she examined the girl who was lifeless again.

"I swear she did," she said softly.

The nurse walked around the bed to Aubrie who had begun to cry and guided her to the door.

"You need a break, why don't we call your foster parents and have them come and get you."

Aubrie bowed her head in sadness and began to walk out the door with the nurse when they heard a gasp from Sydney. They both turned as they watched Sydney's eyes pop open. Before either could reach her, she quickly yanked the breathing tube from her throat.

"Sydney! No!" Aubrie yelled, running back to her.

The nurse rushed to Sydney and called for help. In no time several nurses and doctors were in her room trying to stabilize her while another nurse forced Aubrie from the room.

# # #

Park's party was over and the last of the guests had given their thanks and walked out. All that was left was for Park and Milo to clean up the mess.

"That went very well," Park proudly said as he began picking up plastic cups and stacking them.

"It did. I think you needed that," said Milo.

"Yup and in a couple of days, I'll be under the knife and a step closer to chemo," Park said in high spirits.

"I wish you would have told me that you already knew what was wrong," Milo commented. "I'm your friend, but I get it. Just know that I am gonna be here for you. Will you need me to set up camp here to serve you as you go through the side effects of chemo, maybe hold that long hair of yours while you puke?"

They both laughed before Park became serious.

"Sam's going to help me out," he blurted.

Milo's face brightened and was speechless as Park's phone rang.

Park checked his watch.

"It's almost three in the morning, wonder who that is," he said, walking to the end table in the living room and looking at the name of the caller. "It's Aubrie. I hope she's okay."

Park answered his phone. "Hey Aubrie, are you good?" he asked. "Oh hi, yes this is Park, is Aubrie okay?"

"Yes," said the nurse on the other end of the phone. "Aubrie asked me to call you. She cannot talk right now. It's Sydney. She woke for a moment and pulled her tubing out. We were not able to save her. I'm sorry."

Park's eyes widened. "What? No! No! This can't be. Where is Aubrie?"

Milo stood anxiously waiting to find out what happened.

"Her foster parents just arrived, she is with them. But she wanted me to tell you something that only you would understand," she said with a pause. "She said she wanted you to know that Ostar was going to win."

His face went blank. "Thank you," he softly said before ending the call.

Park was devastated, he stumbled to a chair to sit, leaving Milo anxious.

"Park, what the hell happened?" he asked, kneeling in front of him.

"Sydney is dead. She did it. For him. She did it. She killed herself."

"She woke up?"

"She woke up long enough to do what Ostar wanted. She completed her journey, for him," said Park as he stared at the wall. "My blood, it did no good. Which means it wouldn't have worked on Ostar and we have to find another way."

"Ostar is going to get that pen… eventually he will and he will finish his mission. We both know that," Milo stated in fear.

Park stood and walked to the kitchen and opened a cabinet above the stove. He grabbed an old coffee can, opened it, and pulled out the doll, along with a sealed envelope.

"We can't take that chance," Park said, tossing the envelope to him.

"What's this?" Milo curiously asked.

"Insurance papers, accounts, passwords," he nonchalantly replied.

"Whatever you are thinking Park, don't," Milo ordered as he slowly walked to him.

Park slowly turned the doll over and took out the pen with his right hand, raising it to his face.

"Here's what we are going to do," he said as the ink slowly seeped alongside the pen towards his hand.

www.ingramcontent.com/pod-product-compliance
Lightning Source LLC
Chambersburg PA
CBHW021056130626
46552CB00005B/2132

9781736339800